SUNBURNT

Joey Jameson

To my darling Jet, the original sun worshipper...

Prologue

NOW

His thoughts shifted back to that first moment, back to where it all began. If he concentrated long enough he could picture that face perfectly, as if it were directly in front of him—the shape of his eyes, the strong line of his jaw, the curve of his lips as he smiled. He remembered his smell, sweet and yet salty, like something citrusy mixed with the scent of the sea air.

As he closed his eyes and rested his heavy head in his hands, he imagined the sound of his voice, caressing him gently as it washed over him with its deep, liquid tones. How warm it made him feel once. Safe and cared for, like no ill could ever come as long as they were together. How quickly he felt at ease when he was around. A gentle caress of his warm touch on his cool skin was all it took to make the questions and doubts that filled his head slip away like sand through his fingers.

How foolish he had been.

Squeezing his eyes shut, he gritted his teeth together until his whole jaw ached, attempting to shake the images from his head. But the harder he tried, the more resilient they became, like a stain on his thoughts that got darker and darker the more he tried to scrub them clean.

He could feel the all-too-familiar sense of panic rising in his chest as the memories began to flood his consciousness. Still images, like photographs in an album, seemed to litter the ground around him, tumbling from his mind until he was practically drowning in them. Their relationship played itself out before his very eyes and the more he willed it to stop the more feverish the memories became. He balled his hands into fists against his temples and pressed them so hard to his skull he thought his head would implode. The panic was strong now. It began as a tremor in his gut that poisoned his whole frame as it wormed its way upwards, until it grasped his throat and closed in as if squeezing all the air out of the room.

Then, just as his body temperature was reaching boiling point, an unexpected hand on his shoulder yanked him back from the disease of his own thoughts.

His whole body jolted as he raised his eyes, squinting into the harsh light of the hallway in which he sat. A person stood just before him, towering over him in an authoritative stance. The fluorescent lights caught the metal of the person's badge, drawing his gaze south as if entranced by the glimmering effect.

"It's time."

The figure gestured with a weathered hand towards a room across the hall, his stance signalling a less-than-patient nature.

He took a strained breath which burned as it worked its way through his core, and quietly calmed his nerves. The panic subsided slowly as he took in the reality of where he was. Pulling himself from the seat to which he had become glued, he braced himself for what was about to happen next.

As he walked through the doorway he was greeted by a man and a woman who sat behind a long, grey table. The lights were strong and the air was tense.

The woman was the first to speak.

"Please," she said, motioning to the chair across from them. The table was covered with an array of manila folders arranged neatly in front of them. Their contents were left to his imagination as he moved further into the room and to the lone chair in front of the table.

He heard the heavy door shut behind him and lock as he sat down carefully, at once feeling uneasy and self-conscious. Looking up into the eyes of the man and woman across from him, he felt vulnerable and small, like a mouse in a cage facing his attacker. The room was cold and sterile and void of any emotion, which seemed to suit the situation perfectly. Their eyes burned into him in expectant fashion, as if assessing the situation before he had a chance to even utter a word. The silence was heavy but soon shattered.

"So," began the man in a voice that was startlingly low, "You know why you're here." His words were more of a statement than a question. "Please begin by telling us about your relationship with the deceased..."

Part One

Lenox

Chapter One

T HEN

"Right, hold it there two secs," Lenox Winter hollered at the leggy model draped across his black 2015 Bentley Continental GTC. "Almost got it..." His face was half-hidden behind the lens of his Nikon D500.

"Mate, we have been out here for almost three hours," the model complained, sighing in the most dramatic and over-the-top tone she could muster.

"I know, I know, we're almost there, hang on for me." He spoke in a reassuring tone, feverishly clicking away as he readjusted his stance and zoomed in to focus on the model's top. "Two more frames and I think. We've. Got it." He finished his work. "You're done. Amazing. Thank you so much, you have no idea."

The model did a slight eye-roll before cracking a smile in his general direction. "I wouldn't be out here in this heat for anyone but you, Lenox."

"And I'm eternally grateful, and you know it. Trust me, if I can score an A grade on this final then it might actually get Professor Stine off my back." Lenox squinted down at the viewing frame as he flicked through the shots he'd taken. "Oh, these are brilliant. Molly, you're a star. Thank you so much. Again."

Molly shimmied over to him and past the growing crowd of people who had apparently slowed on their walk to their desired destination to see what all the fuss was about.

"Don't tease a girl! Lemme see, lemme see!"

Lenox tilted the camera towards her, allowing her a better view. Shielding her face from the sun, she leaned in to inspect his work. She let out a gleefully girly squeal and clapped her hands in delight, signalling her approval.

"Daaamn," she drawled. "Girlfriend is working it."

"Glad you like," Lenox said with a wide, toothy grin. "Right, I gotta upload these quick if I'm gonna meet the deadline. Molly, a pleasure as always."

Lenox took Molly's hand in his and thanked her in the most chivalrous way he could muster by lightly kissing it and giving a slight bow. Molly was also a senior at the University of the Arts in West London where Lenox was studying. Unlike him, she wasn't a photography major, but her high cheekbones and luscious mane of golden curls made her the go-to gal for students like Lenox, who needed a pretty face to bring their work to life.

Molly returned his bow with a curtsy. "The pleasure was all mine, kind sir. Right, go and get 'em, tiger. And let me know what Professor Stine thinks of the final." She turned. "Oh, and aren't you going on holiday tomorrow?" she asked from over her shoulder as she collected her purse from the pavement.

Lenox grinned and relaxed. "Yup, can't wait."

"Ibiza, is it?"

He nodded. "My home away from home!"

"You cocky little shit," she joked as she slapped his arm teasingly. "You going with...What was his name?"

Lenox swallowed and lowered his eyes to the ground. "No, we broke up a couple of weeks ago."

"Oh, I'm so sorry."

"Trust me, it was for the better."

He flashed her a forced grin and shook his head as if to rid it of an emotion that was hanging on.

Molly took the hint and smiled back. "Okay, well, enjoy, Lenox. I'll be thinking of you as I stay here, chained to my laptop, slaving away at my remaining finals."

Lenox watched as she sauntered away, bottom shaking from side to side as she disappeared into the setting sun.

Peering up at the crimson-streaked sky, he wiped at his brow and tucked behind his ear a few strands of shoulder-length, jet-black hair that had escaped from his low-slung man bun.

He closed his eyes and reminded himself that, tomorrow, he would be leaving behind the stresses of these past few weeks to soak up the early summer sun in his favourite little holiday hideaway.

He checked his watch as he packed away his ridiculously expensive camera and swore under his breath.

Five forty-five.

At this rate, there was no way he would be able to shower, eat, and make it to the club before his shift started at eight. The shoot with Molly had taken longer than he'd anticipated and, knowing how long it took him to get ready, it was going to be tight.

With his Nikon safely tucked away in its padded protective case, Lenox climbed behind the wheel of his Bentley, started the engine and began the short drive back to West London.

It was a Friday afternoon in the hottest June recorded in England since the 1950s, and as he pulled his car into the traffic of Oxford Street he found himself at a standstill. The irritation inside him grew by the second as he inched closer and closer to being late.

Adjusting his position in the black faux-leather seats, he sat back and regarded his reflection in the rear-view mirror. Lenox Winter was twenty-six and beautiful. With his naturally raven-coloured hair, dark brows and warm, coffee-hued eyes, there was no denying the attention he demanded when he walked into a room.

Not to mention the stares and glances he received as he sat behind the wheel of his sleek, brand-new, Bentley. As his gaze flitted out the window, from the corner of his eye, he spotted the driver from the car next door studying him intently.

Lenox was equal parts pretty boy and bad boy, with his appealing, effortlessly chic sense of style and tall, svelte frame. But regardless of the attention he got from both men and women, he never let it go to his head. Instead, he was almost uncomfortable talking about it if ever one of his friends brought up the subject of his attractiveness.

Running a hand over his strong, permanently stubbled jaw, he wondered if he could get away with this much scruff for his shift tonight, seeing how the time needed to shave was now bound to be outside his reach.

The feeling of his mobile phone vibrating from the pocket of his spray-on skinny jeans was a welcome distraction from the sound of the blaring horns of rush hour. He reached down and pulled it out, clocking the name on caller ID.

Bambi.

His best friend and partner in crime. Also his flatmate, and possible soulmate if they carried on living what he called the "Will-and-Grace-co-dependent" lifestyle they had been enjoying for the past couple of years.

Putting her on speaker phone, he answered the call and placed the handset in the drinks holder on the dash.

"Hey, hey, Miss Von Dutch, what's up?" he called out to her, his face lighting up into a megawatt smile.

"Hiya, you all right?" she asked, the words drenched in her soft mixture of posh West London and cockney North London.

"Yah, good, thanks, you?"

"Yah, good. Where are you?" Bambi enquired, her voice sounding like she was in the middle of eating something.

"Just driving home now. Shoot ran a bit late."

"You okay?"

"Yeah, 'course. Why wouldn't I be?"

Bambi's silence spoke volumes. "Just checking in with you as promised…" She alluded to the subject he was trying to forget with careful tact; the equivalent of walking on eggshells.

"I'm fine. Really. Don't worry about me," he reassured her.

"How did the shoot go?" she asked.

"Yah, good. I think. I guess we'll see what Stine thinks of it this time."

"I'm sure it's another masterpiece," she gushed down the phone in genuine belief. Bambi was Lenox's biggest fan and supporter. Ever the Disney-film optimist, she lived up to her doe-eyed counterpart's name with her unshakable "sunshine and rainbows" view of life.

Lenox smiled, despite feeling uneasy as to how his photos would be judged. He was in the final semester of his Honours BA in Photography, and his final grade largely relied on the theory project that he had been working on for the past three months straight.

"Well, that remains to be seen, I'm afraid."

"Hey, hey, hey, don't let me hear that negative attitude in your voice, please. You need to have a little more faith, Mr. Winter. And if my constant support and reassurance won't do the trick of soothing your nerves, then you'll just have to leave it up to the healing waters of Ibiza, which you'll be bathing in this time tomorrow!" Bambi simultaneously scolded and reminded him.

"Oh, my freaking God, B. You have no idea how excited I am to get away, and how much I need this holiday." His thoughts strayed from the bumper-to-bumper traffic of London to the white, sandy shores of Ibiza.

Ibiza.

To some who visit, the white isle, as it is known, provides a mere temporary escape from their humdrum daily lives. A getaway of sorts to relax and forget about all their troubles.

But to Lenox, Ibiza was a little bit more.

Lenox, now twenty-six, had been holidaying there since he turned eighteen, and the novelty had never once worn thin. It had become almost like a part of him. His spiritual home where he felt no fear or reservation about being his true self.

Despite the fact that, over the years, the reasons for returning had changed, shifting from clubbing destination to a type of spiritual retreat, one thing remained the same. That was the feeling of safety and warmth he got as soon as he stepped off the plane.

Bambi's voice once again stirred him from his daydream. "Don't even get me started. I'm so in need of a holiday that, given half a chance, I'd swim there tonight if I could!"

"I so wanna ring in sick tonight, B," he whined, shortening her name in the way only he could get away with.

"I know, I know. Me too. But we have too much to plan with the other girls tonight before we meet at the airport tomorrow. It'll fly by, so don't worry, my little raven-haired friend. I'll see you in a few."

With that, they ended the call just as he turned the corner onto Kensington Park Road.

The busy energy of Central London dissolved into a more peaceful, suburban vibe as he reached his beloved Notting Hill.

Lenox and Bambi lived in a two-story brick townhouse right in the heart of Notting Hill, a mere two blocks from the house Lenox grew up in and where his parents still resided. The area was beyond affluent; the playground for London's rich and famous who desired high standards without the noise and pollution of more central parts. On a normal day, it wasn't out of the ordinary to spot the likes of Claudia Schiffer grabbing a latte to-go from the local Starbucks or Stella McCartney walking her dog about Portobello Road.

Although he never liked to talk about his family's wealth, it was common knowledge that Lenox had been born into a life of luxury. His father was a rock and roll star whose fortune was made in the seventies and eighties from a string of best-selling albums. He had retired from touring the globe, having performed to sold-out arenas of thousands for the better part of three decades. His mother was his groupie turned road manager, who had amassed money of her own, thanks to her own family's business background. Following in the footsteps of Sharon and Ozzy Osbourne, Lenox's parents were smart with their money, and instead of blowing it all on expensive goods and meaningless luxuries during their height of fame, they had invested wisely. This had secured themselves, and their only son, a more-than-comfortable nest egg on which to rely for the rest of their days. Nowadays, although he certainly didn't need the money, Lenox's father still enjoyed the occasional guest-appearance or duet with an up-and-coming music star to bring in a little something extra if ever he felt so inclined.

Despite being born with a silver spoon in his mouth, Lenox was taught from the moment he could walk that nothing in life was free and that it was through hard work that you made something of yourself. And it was because of these strong values that when Lenox stepped out from the protective umbrella of his parents' influence when he was of age, he decided he wanted to pay his own bills and, other than a little help in the tuition payment department, live a life outside of his family fortune.

As he pulled into their driveway he parked his Bentley snugly next to Bambi's fire-engine red Audi A5. Their house was an absolute gem, purchased many years ago by Lenox's parents as an investment tool for a fraction of what it would be worth now. Despite it being a family property, Lenox and Bambi still paid full rent. They had been given permission to decorate it to reflect a mixture of Lenox's monochrome tendencies and Bambi's bubblegum-pop-electric tastes. The result was like Yves Klein on acid.

Staring up at it for a moment, he couldn't help but felt a tremor of anxiety sweep through him. Looking up to his window, he was instantly brought back to that night, a mere couple of weeks ago. The wounds were still fresh and the memories showed no signs of fading. If he closed his eyes he could still hear that shrill voice echoing in his head. He drew in a deep breath and began his silent count down from ten, his lips moving as he slowly reached zero, sending the rush of pain and panic down to his toes from where it gripped his core. It subsided as quickly as it had come on.

Lenox burst through the door and kicked off his black ankle boots. He was already half undressed as he reached the top of the stairs.

"Hiya, do you want me to spoon you out some salad?" came Bambi's voice from somewhere in the kitchen.

"No time, got to shower quick. Thanks, though!"

"Don't forget, Del Rey is going to pick us up in about half an hour."

"Half an hour? Why so early?" he shouted back as he unbuckled his trousers and headed into the bathroom.

"Don't you remember? Benz wants the whole team there early tonight for a quick catch-up."

She carried on speaking from downstairs, but her baby doll tone was drowned out by the sound of gushing water coming from their waterfall shower head. Even though time was short, Lenox allowed himself a few moments of self-indulgence as he basked in the warm, cascading stream. It relieved and washed away all the stresses he was holding in his muscular shoulders and back.

He would return to the real world in a moment, but right then and there, nothing existed but him, the water, and the fact that tomorrow he would be on a plane, being whisked away to paradise...

Chapter Two

THEN

Lenox and Bambi worked at one of the most unlikely places you'd ever place two upper-class Londoners such as themselves. For the past three and a half years, Lenox had been the main DJ and Bambi a hostess at the high-class strip club "Sunrise Strip" in Soho. For a gay DJ in his twenties like Lenox, it was an odd but perfect fit. Instead of working in one of the hundreds of gay clubs in the area, where he no doubt would spend most of his time fending off the less-than-subtle advances of drunken eighteen-year-olds looking for a one-night hook-up, being employed at a straight strip joint allowed him to work on his spinning technique and neatly hone his craft. Music was a part of his soul, there was no doubt about that, and while he had never learned to play any instruments, much to the chagrin of his father, he had always been drawn to DJ-ing. When he was behind the decks he was in control, and there was nothing more exhilarating than the feeling of getting a crowd going on a dance floor.

At Sunrise Strip, although people weren't paying to see him spin and he certainly was not the main attraction, he was the backbone of the club. Without him and his music, there would be no vibe. And that was enough to satiate his urge.

For now.

As for Bambi Von Dutch, although she could probably retire and live off her family's fortune at her current ripe old age of twenty-nine if she wanted to, her feet were very secure on the ground and she had her eyes on the prize. In her case, the prize was a degree in fashion design, which she was currently working towards at the same university as Lenox. She brought a little something extra to the table at Sunrise Strip. Not only was she the best hostess to grace a venue this side of the Thames, but she also designed and created most of the outfits the girls wore on stage.

Each night at the club was like a runway show of her latest designs: costumes, negligées, the works. And although she knew that she and her work would never be discovered looking after VIP clients at a place like this, the money was all right, the tips were amazing, and it was a chance to practice her sewing skills. So, in her eyes, it all evened itself out. Lenox would often joke that with a name like Bambi she was living out the ultimate cliché. But regardless of what others thought, she owned it.

As they pulled up outside the club in Del Rey's pink Volkswagen Beetle, it was just gone quarter to eight, making the three of them already fifteen minutes late for their meeting.

"Guys, I'm *soooooo* sorry," Del Rey drawled in her raspy cigarette-tinged tone. "I'll totally tell Benz it was all my fault."

Lenox and Bambi shared a subtle eye-roll, as Del Rey's tardiness was nothing new and certainly not unexpected. Del Rey was a dancer at the club, and the personification of the term "sex on two legs." With dark hair extensions that stretched down to her bottom and Double D breasts which were always on display, she did nothing to dispel the stereotype of what a stripper looked and acted like. However, out of herself, Bubbles and Tulip, two of the other dancers at the club who Lenox and Bambi hung around with, she was the most down to earth. Although she could be materialistic and erred slightly on the side of slutty, she was someone you could count on when needed. Lenox knew she would always have his back.

"Don't worry about it. I already texted him saying we were with you and that we would catch up on what was missed when we got there," Lenox reassured her.

"Aww, Lenox, you're an absolute *dollll.*" She made a pouty face as she looked back at him in her rear-view mirror and put the car into park.

They got out of the car and made their way into the building from the rear entrance reserved purely for the dancers and staff. Lenox caught a profile of Del Rey from behind, her long raven-coloured hair swaying from side to side as she walked.

"Jesus, Del Rey, do you actually own any underwear?" he remarked, noticing their absence despite her illicitly short skirt.

"I do, actually. I just...prefer not to wear them."

THE THREE OF them snuck into the very informal meeting just as Benz, the boss and owner of Sunrise Strip, was finishing up his talk. He stood atop a chair, making him appear more giant-like than he normally was.

Nothing about the place was what you'd expect from a London strip club. Including Benz. Besides the fact that he was gay and owned a strip club for straight men, he was also the best boss a stripper could ask for because he actually cared for his dancers like they were his daughters. He had the stature of a bouncer and was made of nothing but muscle. His long blond hair flowed down past his shoulders and his skin was permanently tanned, as if he had forever just returned from a holiday abroad.

"He's a major VIP, so please treat him as such. Regardless of how much of an asshole he tries to be." Benz continued his speech, clocking the three latecomers out of the corner of his eye and trying to hide the annoyance that flashed across his face. "Right, have a good night, everyone." He stepped off the chair on which he was perched and quickly made his way over to the three of them. "You guys all right?" he asked, his eyes searching theirs in a way that emanated genuine concern.

Bambi was the first to speak up, "Sorry we're late…"

"It's my fault," Del Rey interrupted. "First I slept through my alarm, then—"

But Benz simply raised his right hand, signalling to them that excuses weren't necessary. "You're here now, so we're all good," he said, closing his eyes in that very zen way that had an instantly calming effect on all those who came in contact with him. The three of them waited until he opened them again, knowing better than to interrupt him before he was ready to speak. Nothing about Benz ever emanated stress. He was the epitome of serenity and calm, despite owning and managing a high-profile London club. When he finally opened his eyes, it was as if he had just returned from somewhere deep in his own mind, having gathered his thoughts. As he opened his mouth to speak, his expression had shifted once again, indicating he was now all about business.

"Right. Lenox, we need high energy tonight. Especially since our VIP guest owns a number of the top hotels in Vegas. He's heard about us and is here to check out the scene and possibly invest if he likes what he sees, so I need you to be on top of your game tonight."

Lenox nodded, and Benz winked at him.

"Bambi, I need your eyes to be constantly on his section," he went on. "If he looks in need of anything I want you on it even before he raises his eyes to ask. Understand?"

"Got it."

"Del Rey," Benz began, looking her up and down quickly and taking in her appearance, which verged on the obscene for this time of night.

"Yeah, boss?" she asked, her large, surgically enhanced lips smacking away at a piece of pink bubblegum.

"You just do what you do best up there on stage."

BY TEN O'CLOCK, the club was full to capacity. The VIP area was overflowing into the main stage area due to the hotel mogul from Las Vegas, whose party seemed to be multiplying by the minute.

The girls on stage were on fire, shaking it and working every last seat in the room with a hunger Lenox had never seen before. The energy in the club was charged as, dance after dance, Lenox delivered banging tracks that seemed to breathe new life into the dancers, taking hold of their bodies and twisting them to his will.

This was what he was good at. Lenox could read vibes and knew just what to mix in at what time to keep the audience engaged and the girls pumped. If heads started to look away in the crowd, then he knew he had to kick it up into high gear to keep those eyes locked on the girls. He remained engaged with the dancers, watching them and reading their movements, sensing what they needed and delivering it to them in the form of his tracks. When the clothes hit the floor, his job was only halfway done. He needed to take things home and stick with it until the last second.

Or last twirl on the pole, as the case may be.

Lenox was giving it everything he could to keep the energy up, aware of the watchful gaze of Benz, who never seemed to stray too far from sight, keeping an eye directed towards the VIP area. But Lenox had to focus hard to stay in the game tonight, for each time he played a new track he couldn't help but imagine he was already on holiday. If he closed his eyes long enough and let the beat wash through him he could almost feel the sand between his toes and the Ibizan sun on his face.

Just before midnight, and between dances, Bambi rounded up Del Rey, Tulip and Bubbles and brought a round of Porn Star shots to Lenox in the DJ booth. The five of them had grown closer and closer since meeting at the club almost four years ago, and despite looking like characters from *The Island of Misfit Toys* when they went out together, they each brought something special to the friendship.

Lenox was the dreamer, forever with his head in the clouds, while Bambi was the responsible one, making plans and always very methodical in her thinking. Del Rey played up to how people viewed her as the sexy tomcat, while Bubbles was the ditz, right down to her blonde ringlets and high-pitched East-London-meets-Valley-girl voice. Then there was Tulip, who gave new meaning to the label "wild child."

But regardless of their differences, when they were together, everyone got along.

"Right, ladies and gent, this time tomorrow we will be trashed and dancing the night away!" Bambi shouted over the thumping bassline, raising a shot glass in the air.

"Aren't we trashed and dancing the night away right *now*?" Tulip shouted back, her wide mouth open in an ear-to-ear grin.

"Yes, but tomorrow we'll be doing it in *fucking Ibiza, baby!*" Del Rey countered, tipping the shot glass back and downing hers prematurely.

"*Oi*, you're supposed to wait for us!" Bubbles giggled before following suit and swallowing hers in one big gulp.

"You're all ruining my cheers," Bambi moaned, only half-serious.

"Oh shut up, B, and drink your drink!" Lenox joked, touching his shot gently to hers and meeting her gaze before tossing back the fruity liquid and slamming the glass down on the black marble counter that surrounded his decks.

"Is everything sorted with the villa?" Bambi asked, a flash of concern shadowing her wide-eyed and innocent features.

"Yes, yes, yes, don't worry your pretty little head," Tulip said with a dramatic eye-roll.

"You're sure?"

"Yes, Bambi."

"You're sure you're sure?" she asked again for emphasis, a smile tugging at her full lips.

"Are you for real?" Tulip joked back. "Yes, I'm sure. My uncle said we can enjoy his villa for the whole week. The keys will be left with his cleaning lady, who will meet us outside at noon. And we can even take out the jet skis if we want!"

"*What*? He's got jet skis? For real?" Lenox asked, his face lighting up.

"Yup. There's a little dock just down from the guest house, so we have our own private launch pad, if we so desire."

"Yes, we so desire!"

"I thought you might. This is going to be the most killer holiday. I can't freakin' wait!" Del Rey shouted back.

The group let out a chorus of whoops as the bass picked up and spiked into an incredible drop that had all their asses shaking around the booth. For a moment, they all lost themselves in the music as they closed their eyes and let their bodies move to the beat. The sound of the drum and bass hammered the air around them, piercing it with its rhythmic sway and relentless hold. Lenox opened his eyes for a moment to adjust the monitor volume on the decks and noticed someone standing and staring at them about fifty feet away.

He strained his eyes to focus, finding it odd that someone could be drawing attention from the girls on the stage, but the flashing strobe lights made the figure's shadow dance and shake to the point where their face remained in darkness. Lenox stilled for a moment and closed his eyes tightly before opening them and looking again, hoping it was all a trick of the lights and the booze making him see things. But the shape was still there.

He instantly thought it was *him*. He must have followed Lenox to work.

How long has he been watching me?

It was the eerie stillness with which the person stood, hands resting limply at their sides, that drew his attention.

So still. Unmoving.

Lenox reached out for Bambi and pulled her out of the dancing circle.

"B, it's—"

Bambi looked at Lenox and followed his gaze to the empty space in front of him.

"What? What is it, Lenox?"

"I thought I saw…"

But the shape was gone.

Bambi must have recognised the signs of Lenox's rising panic. She placed a hand on his shoulders and stood directly in front of him, trying to gain control of the situation.

“Look at me, Lenox. I’m here. You’re okay. You’re safe.” She spoke each short sentence in an assured tone that worked to calm him in the way she had been taught.

“I’m good. Thank you. Sorry.”

Bambi led him back towards his group of friends. Lenox caught her stealing a look behind her, just in case.

Chapter Three

Now

"Could you please state your name for the record."

The woman's voice was less than feminine, tinged with a lilting Spanish accent, and reminded him of the way steel would sound if it could speak.

He returned her question with silence, his eyes staring intently down at his balled-up fists which were nestled tightly in his lap. The room was quiet with the only noises being a ticking sound coming from the clock on the wall and the humming of the decades-old air conditioning that wasn't doing its job too well anymore.

"Your name?" she tried again, more forcefully this time around—if that were even possible. Her irritating tone jarred him from his thoughts and he peered up at her from behind his long lashes.

"You know my name." His tone was clipped and void of any emotion.

The woman shifted in her chair, but her eyes never left his face. Her partner remained fixed in place, unmoving and unfazed by his unwillingness to cooperate.

"Perhaps you weren't made aware of the seriousness of this situation."

"Am I being charged?" he asked. But he already knew the answer to that and the silence from the officers only confirmed his suspicions. His lips lifted into a smug smile as his eyes drifted back down to his hands.

The female officer proceeded to sift through the envelopes on the table, taking out photographs in hopes of jarring a certain reaction from him. But his eyes didn't shift as she had hoped. Their colour seemed drained and dull, as if faded somehow. Even his skin had lost its summer glow and appeared almost grey in the fluorescent lighting.

"We're investigating the deaths of four individuals. All young men under the age of thirty."

Her hands flitted over four A4 photographs that she adjusted carefully on the table like images from some grotesque shopping catalogue.

Her partner leaned in, placed his forearms on the table that separated them, and steepled his hands under his chin. The officer's sudden movement caused him to look up quickly.

"Sir, apparently—" He paused on the word. "We have reasonable grounds to suspect your involvement in numerous indictable offences, involving one case of manslaughter and three of murder." The officer's tone was direct and forceful, but questioning at the same time as if he himself didn't believe his accusation.

He fought a slight lip quiver, praying that the officers hadn't noticed his reaction. The smugness gone, he opened his mouth to respond but no words came out.

"Well. It looks like we have your attention now…"

Chapter Four

THEN

That night, Lenox dreamed of white sand and peaceful vibes. In the morning, he showered quickly, finished the last of his packing, and set off in an Uber cab for Gatwick Airport.

On the flight, he sat between Bambi and Bubbles, with Del Rey and Tulip occupying the seats across the aisle. They toasted their holiday with champagne and nibbles, despite it only being early afternoon. After polishing off two bottles of Moët between the five of them, they arrived in the Balearic Isles.

To Lenox, it never felt real until he stepped off the plane and felt the dry, blistering air of the Mediterranean on his skin. That was when it hit him. He had arrived in his little piece of paradise.

Ibiza.

As he closed his eyes and breathed in, the stresses of the last few months began to melt away from his shoulders. His final project had been turned in and now that the incident with his ex was hopefully over and done with, he could finally relax.

The tension that he kept in his back began to lessen as they boarded the shuttle bus for the arrivals lounge and he was filled with a newfound sense of ease and simplicity.

Lenox had been coming to Ibiza for as long as he could remember. It was his parents' holiday destination of choice. They would venture over as often as they could, claiming there was something about the energy of the small island that kept them coming back year after year. They taught their only son about the history of the island and how to respect it when he came, being sure to abide by the ways of the locals and to leave his accommodation in the same condition as he found it. Despite their connection with the land, they would fluctuate their stays between lavish resorts and hotels like the Grand Palladium or The Can Lluc, where they would receive five-star service and be waited on hand and foot, and more demure and quaint locations where it was just them, the sea, and the sand.

Lenox quickly learned that authentic Ibiza lay away from the pampered experiences of the rich and famous, where you could mingle with the natives, swim on lesser-known beaches, and experience the real energy that Ibiza offered to those who walked on its shores.

When he turned eighteen, he visited for the first time without his parents and saw the island from a new perspective. He remembered his mother's words as he found his way among the windy hills and dusty roads, being sure to respect everything and everyone he came in contact with. Although he was no stranger to the wild nights that Ibiza had to offer, these days, as he approached the end of his twenties, he much preferred the chilled holiday experience.

The temperatures in Ibiza were unforgiving. He and his friends made their way through Arrivals and collected their cases, then hopped in a waiting private-hire van and were off.

Lenox's phone pinged and he reached down to pull it out of his back pocket.

"Did you tag us here already, B?"

"You know it!"

Bambi was never one to let anything be left to the unknown. She was what Lenox deemed to be a "social media hussy," always posting lurid pictures of herself and all willing parties when out and about, and a holiday abroad was high time to show off to her thousands of followers the mischief she was bound to get up to.

"Ugh, when did you take that photo?" Lenox scoffed at his iPhone screen.

"What? Lemme see!" Bubbles demanded, getting closer to the screen.

"What? It's a candid photo!" Del Rey chimed in.

"You can practically see the drool dripping from my bottom lip!" Lenox whined at the photo of him snoozing on the flight and the rest of the girls wrapped around him adoringly as he slept, completely oblivious to the selfie being taken.

"You look lovely, my darling," Del Rey added.

"Fuck," Lenox said under his breath.

"What's wrong?" Del Rey asked.

Lenox turned the phone so she could see the comments below.

In big capital letters, was the word CUNT.

Lenox didn't need to look any further to see who had written it. He knew immediately who the message was from.

Del Rey looked from the phone to him and quickly, in the way that she was so well versed, went on the defence. "Is that from...? Shit. I'm deleting it."

"I thought we all blocked him?" Bambi said quickly.

"Shit. I'm sorry. I thought I had..."

The girls all checked their phones and searched for the relevant details to make sure he was on their list of blocked contacts.

"I'm so sorry, Lenox."

Lenox's eyes were unfocused as he stared out the window.

"It's done. There. Blocked and I've deleted the comment. It's fine." Del Rey's usually calm tone was shaky as she put her phone back in her bag and crossed her arms over her chest.

The van was quiet for a few minutes as the reality of the situation settled in, the vibe shifting from calm to tense in a matter of moments. Bambi put a hand on Lenox's leg reassuringly.

"It's okay, Lenox. Really," she said in hushed tones.

"He knows where I am now, B..." Lenox whispered.

But Bambi didn't respond; instead, she squeezed his knee.

Lenox drew in a deep breath, somewhat jarred and on edge all of a sudden. The hairs on the back of his neck prickled and his throat dried up.

They continued on down the road for a minute or so before Tulip's harsh tone interrupted the silence. "Bloody hell, I can't believe how hot it is!" she stated from the front passenger side seat.

"What did you expect, you saw how balmy it was in the UK, didn't ya?" Del Rey countered, fanning herself with a foldaway fan as if she was a film star from the twenties.

"I know, but I'm sweating my tits off up here. Any chance you can crank up the A.C., mate?" she asked the driver, who only looked at her eyes briefly before his gaze lowered to Tulip's enormous cleavage which appeared buttery smooth in the early afternoon sun. "Hiya, mate. I'm up *here!*" she yelled, only half serious, clicking her fingers to divert his attention from her boobs.

The whole group laughed heartily, thankful for the break in tension. Even Lenox eased up slightly, his face cracking into a wide grin as he took in the situation. There was nothing he could do to change what had just happened. He drew in a deep breath and tried to convince himself that it really would be okay.

"What do you expect, hun? The girls are commanding everyone's attention today," Lenox said as he raked a hand through his thick black hair, sweeping it off his sticky forehead. "I'm afraid to say that I can barely take my eyes off them, and I'm about as queer as they come!"

It felt good to laugh. This was exactly what Lenox needed and one of the reasons they had all planned this holiday in the first place.

"Well, if you're starting to zero in on boobs these days, then I'm thinking there is no better time than the present to find you some *dick!*" Tulip threw back at him, causing the car to erupt once more into a series of catcalls at Lenox's expense. "And I mean some good dick. Not some crazy-ass dick like the last fool, but some good old-fashioned *sane* dick."

"Yeah, yeah, like I'd ever let a ho like you play matchmaker for me."

"Uh, excuse me? Who you callin' a ho?"

"I'm just saying. When's the last time *you* had a boyfriend?"

"Who said anything about *boyfriends?*" Tulip asked, twirling a finger through her short crimson bob. "I'm just saying it's time we got you laid!"

"She's right, Lenox. Sometimes all you need to get over one guy…" Bubbles began.

"*Is to get under another one!*" the girls chorused together, before erupting into a fit of high-pitched giggles.

"Trust me, I don't need to *try* to get over this one. I need to bloody *forget* about him," he said, trying to make light of the situation.

Lenox averted his gaze and peered out the window, knowing despite his retort that they were right. After what happened he knew it would take a lot before he could trust someone again. Watching the rolling hills of the Ibizan countryside pass by outside his window, he inwardly castigated himself for not seeing the signs or taking notice of the red flags that had shown themselves so regularly in his last relationship.

If he closed his eyes long enough he could still see his face with that look of rage plastered across it. If he concentrated hard enough he could still hear the crack of his ribs as he was kicked repeatedly, or the steely taste of blood in his mouth that he thought would never go away. Never had he experienced such anger and violence from someone before. Now all he could do was pray every night that it was over.

Bambi patted his knee in a slightly condescending manner, bringing his attention back to the van.

"Tulip's right, actually. You have been spending quite a bit of time lately either holed up in your darkroom or surrounded by strippers and rowdy straight men," she remarked, almost reading his thoughts. "Maybe it is time you got yourself back out there."

"What, on holiday?"

"Yes, on holiday! Specifically, on holiday!"

Lenox only shook his head. "A holiday romance isn't what I need right now." He returned his eyes to the views outside his window.

"Uhhh, hands up if you disagree with Lenox."

He turned to see Del Rey raising her hand firmly in the air. The rest of the ladies raised a hand each in turn.

"Oh, come on! What's the point? Anything that happens while away isn't gonna last..."

"That *is* the point, my raven-haired friend! It's the perfect scenario, because you know you're leaving!" Bambi purred, flashing him a wink.

"I believe what you're referring to is 'expiration dating.'"

"There you go again with that *dating* crap," Tulip argued, putting the word in-between air quotations. "It doesn't have to be dating. It's sex. Good old-fashioned holiday-abroad sex. Shake off that stalker-y mojo you've been dragging around with you."

Lenox returned his gaze to the window and tucked his hands tightly away in his lap.

"Listen to your friends for once, Lenox. We're on holiday. You never know what might happen!" Bambi proposed, planting a seed in the air around them.

As the countryside began to disperse and the landscape became littered with resorts and billboards advertising club nights and DJs, Lenox let their words wash through him. He allowed himself to consider, just for a moment, if there was some truth behind them.

Chapter Five

THEN

The villa belonged to Tulip's uncle, who had purchased the property sometime in the early nineties, well before the recession and before Ibiza saw an influx of tourists attracted by the rave movement of the time. It was classically designed with whitewashed walls and a minimalist feel to its five-bedroom layout. Despite being relatively new compared to other properties on the island, it had recently been refurbished and modernised, including the addition of an enormous infinity pool which allowed for the most breathtaking view of the area between Figueretas beach and Playa D'en Bossa.

The bedrooms were interconnected and simple, furnished with king size beds and walk-in wardrobes, and enormous bay windows that opened up onto a balcony that stretched the entire width of the apartment.

On their first full day on the island, Lenox woke up to the warm early morning sun streaming in through the windows, caressing his face with its gentle movement as it swept slowly through the room. The windows were open, letting in a whistling gust of fresh air that ruffled the floor-to-ceiling white silk curtains. Lenox breathed in the rejuvenating early summer breeze, tossed back the thin cotton duvet, and practically leaped out of bed.

As the years passed, Lenox had made a silent promise to himself not to waste the precious Ibizan days hung-over or strung out in bed, but instead to embrace his time on the island by taking in all of it he could. Within moments of being out of bed, he was dressed and feeling the soft caress of the bleached white sand between his toes.

He loved this time of day in Ibiza. The sun was just starting to show itself in the sky above the tall lookout tower of the D'Alt Villa, its already warm rays heating up the sand at his feet. Here and there, he spotted the occasional local, out for their morning stroll along the otherwise deserted beaches, or swimming slowly through the warm waters. He smiled at those he passed, the skin crinkling at the corners of his dark eyes as he did, his feet treading through the surf where the water met the sand. He held out his phone to capture the pink sky before continuing on his way. His thoughts were slowed and his stresses few as he closed his eyes for a moment and took it all in.

His blissed-out thoughts were momentarily disturbed as the soft sound of what he presumed was a guitar being played reached his ears. Lenox turned his head in the direction of the gentle strumming. As he took another few steps and craned his neck to see beyond the array of beach chairs and umbrellas, he spotted where the sound was coming from.

A man sat on one of the long beach chairs, incredibly tanned legs outstretched and clutching what turned out to be a ukulele gently in his arms. The sight of him caught Lenox off-guard and he slowed his pace to get a better look.

To say he was beautiful would be the understatement of the century. His skin was the colour of golden butter and appeared just as smooth. He was shirtless, wearing nothing but board shorts that rode up slightly and exposed the muscles in his thighs as he crossed his legs in front of him. He had neatly done sun-kissed dreadlocks that grazed just below his tanned and round nipples. As his fingers worked the strings on the ukulele, he hummed and murmured a beautiful accompaniment; something almost pained or tortured yet soulful at the same time, as if playing the instrument was his deliverance from whatever conflict he faced. The notes dusted the air gently as they danced all around him, hitting the waves and bouncing back towards where Lenox stood, dumbfounded and entranced by the sweet, melodic music.

He could do nothing but stare, his mouth a little ajar and his heart picking up speed as his eyes drank in the sight of this tanned Adonis before him. He was like nothing Lenox had ever seen back in London, and the more Lenox stared the more he was filled with a sense of ease. The air around him was heavy with a mixture of sex appeal and desire. Lenox thought perhaps it was the gentle sound of the ukulele, or maybe the way the stranger's voice echoed against the surrounding mountains, but he was certainly overcome with a sense of allure which manifested as a stirring in his stomach like a thousand butterflies, flapping madly to get out.

It took a moment for the man to realise he was being watched but as he turned his aqua-coloured eyes turned towards Lenox, their pained expression gently relaxed into a slight smile that was at once a gesture of acknowledgement and thanks to his unexpected audience.

Lenox felt very self-aware and didn't know where to look. His eyes cast downwards to his toes and his body began to move awkwardly as if he was searching for something in the sand. The gentle humming and sound of the instrument continued as Lenox began moving away from it. He swallowed hard as regret and frustration flooded his psyche, the words of his friends repeating themselves in his ear.

Maybe it is time you get yourself out there...

But as he found himself wandering further and further away, the beautiful music growing dimmer and dimmer, he felt the moment escape him.

LENOX AND THE girls spent the day sunning themselves on the beautiful Playa D'en Bossa. The sun was hot and the water not much cooler as they let the energies of the island filter through them, awakening their every nerve and invigorating their souls. The traffic and noise of London seemed a million miles away, as the lapping sounds of the turquoise waters wrapped them in a warm, protective cocoon.

Bambi and Bubbles could lie in the sun all day, applying and reapplying Hawaiian Tropic tanning oil to their already deep hued skin, but Tulip and Del Rey got restless easily.

"Can we go check out Bora Bora soon?" Tulip asked, the question coming out dipped in a childish whine. "I can hear the beats from here and they're making me antsy."

"Gimme ten more minutes. I just need to turn over then I'll be ready," Bambi said, not once tilting her face from the direct line of the sun above.

"Girl, you're already the colour of a cross between an extra from *The Real Housewives* and freakin' Donatella Versace!"

"Good, that's exactly the look I was going for."

"Bubbles, what about you?" Del Rey asked.

"Why don't you two go ahead and we'll meet up with you?"

"Lenox, what are you feeling?" Bubbles squeaked in his general direction, only to be greeted with silence. "Lenox? *Oi!* Lenox, you with us?" she repeated, gently slapping his arm to break him from his trance. He had his head inside his beach bag as he searched manically for his phone.

"What you looking for, Lenox?"

"Sorry, what?" he responded, coming back from where he was.

"You all right, mate? You seem miles away..." Del Rey remarked.

"Yeah, all good. Sorry, I can't find my phone. What did you say?"

"Did you leave it back at the villa?"

"I dunno. I'm sure I had it in here. Can someone ring it for me?"

Bambi picked up her phone and dialled. Everyone listened for a minute for the sound of it ringing, but there was nothing.

"Fuck. I bet I lost it on the beach this morning."

"Don't worry. You got a password on it, right?"

"No. You know I hate having to punch it in every time."

"Seriously, mate? You don't have a password on it?" Tulip mocked.

"That's really fucking helpful, Tulip," he shot back.

"Don't worry, it'll turn up. It's probably back at the villa. We'll check as soon as we get in," Bambi said complacently.

Lenox just sighed and looked out to sea, inwardly beating himself up for being so absentminded.

Tulip and Del Rey gave each other a look and started to move.

"Well we're gonna hit up Bora Bora down the beach for some drinks, you wanna come with?" Tulip interjected, standing and draping her tiny frame in a hooded beach wrap.

"Uhh, actually, I think I'll just chill here a bit longer. You staying?" He motioned to Bambi, who nodded in response.

"Right, you lot have fun then. We're going to get drinks."

"And maybe some blokes!" Tulip joked.

"Don't even think about bringing any randoms back, ladies. Remember we have dinner reservations at nine," Bambi scolded.

"Hey, if no one else around here is interested in getting some, then I might as well. We're on holiday, aren't we?" Tulip said.

They all blew air kisses to each other before Tulip and Del Rey scuttled away down the beach.

As soon as they were out of earshot, Bambi turned to Lenox, lowering her sunglasses so she could stare him straight in the eye. Lenox did a double take upon feeling her sensors taking him down before lowering his own shades to meet her gaze.

"Penny for your thoughts, Mister Winter?" she asked coquettishly.

"Whatever do you mean, Miss Von Dutch?" He toyed with her.

"Don't feign innocence with me, Lenox. What's on your mind? You okay?"

Lenox glanced away for a moment and pretended to look for something further down the beach.

Bubbles seemed to sense the tension in the air and sat up abruptly to better take in the situation. "What'd I miss?"

"Lenox is about to reveal a secret, I can tell!"

"You're so wrong, I'm afraid. Nothing much to tell..."

"Nothing *much?* So, you admit, there *is* something!"

"Hardly..." He looked away to avoid the girls' penetrative stares.

"Come on, Lenox, what is it?" Bubbles asked, getting in on the game.

Lenox took another moment before sighing heavily. "Oh, fuck it. This morning. On the beach..."

"You went to the beach this morning?" Bambi interrupted.

"Not the point of the story!"

"Sorry. Continue."

"So, I went to the beach as the sun was coming up—"

"Oh, my God, we're getting so old!" Bubbles exclaimed, once again halting Lenox's story in its tracks. "Remember the good old days when we would still be out when the sun was coming up?"

Lenox didn't respond. Neither did Bambi. Instead, they just stared at her from over the rims of their sunglasses.

"Sorry. Did it again. Please, go on..."

"Anyways. There's not much to tell." Lenox shrugged. "But when I was walking...I saw this guy..."

"Ooh, really? What's his name?" Bambi asked quickly.

"Was he cute?" Bubbles jumped in again.

"What's he look like?" Bambi said.

"Well, I don't...I mean, I didn't..."

"Didn't what? Is he staying close by?" Bambi shot back quickly.

"I don't know..."

"What do you mean you don't know? What did you say to him?"

The questions were coming quickly now, like wild fire; faster than he could muster up his pathetic response.

"Actually, I didn't say...Anything..."

"What? Why not?"

"I...I don't know. I just, kept on walking..."

The girls were finally quiet as they took in Lenox's inherent shyness and the sad reality of the situation.

"Oh," Bambi said, a full stop quite apparent in her tone.

Lenox studied their faces and saw the two girls make eye contact quickly and sheepishly. "What? Oh, go on, say it."

There was another silent exchange between the girls before Bambi opened her mouth to speak.

"I think I speak for both Bubbles and I when I say 'typical Lenox'..."

"*Typical Lenox*? What's that supposed to mean?"

"It means that chickening out in the presence of a good-looking guy is typically you!"

"I don't chicken out in front of guys..."

This time both ladies shot him a double dose of a look that said *really?*

"Well, I don't do it often...And who are you both to talk?" He gestured towards them both in a less-than-subtle way to redirect the topic of conversation away from himself.

"No, no, no, don't even try to deflect," Bambi countered, shaking a finger in his direction.

"Well, you must at least remember something about what he looked like?" Bubbles said, gently coming to his rescue.

Lenox looked out to sea for a moment as he thought of how best to describe the man from earlier.

"Well, he had these beautiful, long blond dreads—"

"*Dreadlocks?*" Bubbles shot back.

"Really, Lenox? Dreads? Since when do you like dreads on a guy?"

"Right. I knew I should have kept my mouth shut. Never mind. Forget I said anything."

Lenox stood up abruptly and brushed the sand off his shorts before grabbing his towel to leave.

"Lenox, come on. We're just teasing you. Really. Sit down and tell us more about your dreaded friend," Bambi joked, high-fiving Bubbles without diverting her gaze from Lenox.

"Yeah, don't be such a prissy pants. Sit, tell us more."

But Lenox had made up his mind. And as much as it was a tad on the dramatic side, his sudden self-awareness and vulnerability had given him cause to leave.

"I'm gonna go. I'll catch you both back at the villa."

"Lenox, don't. Come on, we're just joking."

"It's all good. I'll see you later."

He grabbed his flip-flops and turned to go.

Chapter Six

THEN

Lenox was in a funk for the rest of the afternoon. After he deserted Bambi and Bubbles, he found himself walking down the same stretch of beach as that morning in the hope of locating his now officially missing phone. But also in the hope of spotting the music guy again. A vain sense of optimism tickled his insides as he searched the throngs of people gathered around umbrellas. He inwardly scolded himself when disappointment flooded through him as he realised there was no "mystery man" to be seen. And no phone. He sighed but made a mental plan to give it at least another day before going online and reporting his handset as missing. He'd be phone-free for the rest of the holiday, which was inconvenient to say the least, but would get a replacement, and perhaps a well-needed upgrade, when he got back to the UK.

After a quick swim on the less-crowded Figueretas beach, he returned to the villa to have a nap and get himself ready for dinner with the girls.

Their reservation was at Las Dos Lunas, one of the island's swankiest and most iconic restaurants near San Rafael. Lenox remembered visiting with his parents when he was younger and sitting opposite who he would learn to be Mick Jagger, only one of the many celebrities who visited the posh establishment on a regular basis.

Tonight's crowd was a mixture of posh Ibiza locals and bohemian beauties, draped in colourful layers of sheer fabric and jewels that caught the vibrant overhead lights of the restaurant, casting glittery shadows on the walls. But as much as the patrons themselves rivalled the glitterati of London, the ambience and vibe within was true Ibizan, laid-back couture. The hushed tones of the diners were blanketed by the deep house music grooves that came from the DJ booth at the front of the room, creating a melodic atmosphere that complemented the decor beautifully.

As Lenox and his friends dined on small plates of chargrilled eggplant, gratin of mussels, and gnocchi gorgonzola, and drank bottle after bottle of Campillo and Marqués de Arienzo, their conversation flowed just as easily. There was no denying how busy their lives had become as of late; juggling working late nights with early morning classes, so for them to get together outside of the club and on their own terms was a rare occurrence.

Being outside London was a chance to soak up what the rest of the world had to offer. Sometimes, living in the belly of England's capital city caused Lenox to feel claustrophobic and stifled by the fast pace and constant influx of information and sensory overload. Ibiza provided the antithesis to his daily routine and was the perfect medicine that he gladly would drink by the bottle if he could.

At some point, Lenox became aware that the wait staff had begun to tidy up, moving chairs around him and his friends. They were the last remaining patrons of the evening, and this was an obvious attempt to signal to them that it was well beyond last call.

A quick glance at his watch showed it was indeed after one-thirty in the morning.

"Shit, guys, where did the time go?" Lenox said.

"Why, what time is it?" Bambi asked.

"Gone half one,"

"What? Really? But we're just getting started!" Del Rey whined.

A man dressed in the seemingly universal wait staff attire of white shirt and black trousers came over and signalled with his head towards the front of the restaurant.

"*Los taxis están al frente,*" he whispered under his breath.

Lenox had taken A Level Spanish before he left school and remembered enough to know that the waiter had just said that the cabs were out front.

The girls looked at Lenox for a bit of help as their expressions told him they were lost in translation.

"He's basically telling us to get the fuck out!" Lenox joked, downing the remaining wine in his tall glass.

"Right, finish up, ladies!" Bambi ordered, ever the group organiser.

"Where to now then, kids?" Tulip asked, wrapping her leopard-print half-wrap around her otherwise bare shoulders.

"We're fairly close to Amnesia," Bubbles said hopefully.

"I'm not sure I'm up for a club night tonight…" Lenox countered.

"Whaaaat? Why not?" Bubbles whined.

"How's about we keep this party going down on the beach?" Lenox threw the suggestion out there, his eyes searching their reactions. "Maybe grab a couple bottles of fizz from the all-night shop, then drinks on the beach…And take the rest of the night from there?"

The girls exchanged silent glances as the wait staff busied themselves around the empty tables.

"I promise it'll be fun."

Lenox was all wide eyes and cheeky smiles, putting on his best puppy dog face in a last-ditch attempt to get what he wanted.

As much as he was trying to hide it from the group, he hadn't been able to get the sexy, ukulele-strumming guy from the beach out of his head all day. Secretly, a part of him hoped that he might run into him again. But even as he waited for his friends to respond to his lame attempt to deter them from a club night, he realised how ridiculous he was being. Despite the small size of the island, the chances of his running into someone he'd only glanced from afar once, at the start of tourist season on the party island capital of the world, were slim to none.

Chapter Seven

THEN

Despite the girls' initial hesitation to go along with Lenox's suggestion of bubbles on the beach, within the hour they had freshened up, grabbed a couple of blankets from the villa to sit on and stocked up on four bottles of Spanish Cava from their local shop.

Giggling and talking at a volume that was attracting disapproving stares from others out for romantic, late-night strolls along the beach, they made their way towards the water's edge. Lenox couldn't help but scan the shadowed faces along the beach, but as far as he could tell, there were no signs of any dreadlocks in sight.

As the bottles were popped and the sound of trickling alcohol being tipped into tall flutes hit his ears, Lenox's distracted glances caught Bambi's eye.

"What?" he asked sheepishly, knowing she could see right through his innocent facade.

"Looking for someone?" she countered.

"What do you mean?"

But Bambi only smiled coquettishly and nodded, her eyes narrowing as she took a spot on the blanket.

The air was refreshing and cool, with a gentle salty breeze coming off the ocean that caressed their hot skin but left a gritty film in its wake. Lenox shivered despite himself before Del Rey's smoky voice interrupted his thoughts.

"Hey chief, you coming in for a landing?"

Lenox turned away from the sea for a moment to greet her questioning glance before being drawn back towards the sound of someone surfacing from the water just off to his left.

It took a moment for his alcohol-induced double vision to focus enough to see the body climbing out of the sea, and a moment further to register the familiarity of the shape. Something inside him sparked as if a flint had just lit a pile of dried leaves, causing flames to jump and lick the air around them, his body coming to life as he lit up from inside.

He noticed the blond dreads first, then the incredibly toned arms and chest. The moon from above made the water glisten as it ran south over the man's round pectoral muscles. The rushing waves made it seem like he was moving in slow motion as his thick calves fought against the tide, his stride strong as he lifted his knees high in the air to reach the shore. He gave his head a shake from side to side, ridding his dreadlocks of excess water, before he reached up and ran both hands through them, lifting their length from his shoulders before letting them cascade down his back. His solid biceps flexed with the motion before he ran his hands over his frame, wiping droplets of water from his chest and lifting the material of his hot pink swimming trunks that had suctioned itself to his legs.

Lenox could do nothing but gape at the sight as his heart raced with excitement and the butterflies recommitted to their rhythmic beating in his stomach.

It took a moment for the others to turn their attention back to their statue-like comrade, stood erect on the spot, apparently entranced by something in the water. Tulip was the first to take notice.

"Mate, what you on about? You joining us or what?"

"What are you looking at, Lenox?" Del Rey added, her eyes following his deadpan gaze towards the water's edge.

"Yeah, what are you...?" Bubbles started before taking immediate notice and stopping herself in her tracks.

The group erupted into a fit of schoolgirl giggles as they too noticed the beautifully tanned, blond Adonis emerging from the water. Lenox felt like he had been caught with his hand in the cookie jar. He turned to them and sunk to the blanket, eyes wide and face full of embarrassment as he shushed them quickly in hopes that the man wouldn't spot them.

"Oh. My. God!" Bambi declared, much louder than Lenox would have liked. "Is that who I think it is?"

"Shhh!"

"No! Really? Mm-hmm! That boy is fiiiine. Now I see why you wanted to come down to the beach."

"Oh my God, shut up! He'll hear you!"

"Wait a minute, is that the bloke from this morning?" Bubbles asked, forever slow on the uptake.

"Hey, hot stuff, nice abs!" Tulip shouted at the stranger, sounding like a construction worker hollering at a pretty girl on the street.

Lenox averted his gaze from the nightmare playing out in front of him and wished silently he could bury his face in the sand.

"I hate you all!" he whispered through gritted teeth.

"It's okay, Lenox. He's gone. Don't worry," Tulip said.

Relieved, Lenox lifted his head to look in the direction from where he'd spotted his mystery man.

"Psyche!" Tulip teased before erupting into an evil cackle as Lenox realised Tulip's lie.

Lenox dared steal a glance back to the guy who was now wiping himself down, a grin playing with the corners of his mouth as he listened to the teasing and heckling happening to his left. He lifted his head and made eye contact with Lenox for the first time since the previous morning.

The effect was electric.

Despite his utter embarrassment, Lenox couldn't look away. He wasn't sure if he was returning the sly smile directed his way, or staring dumbfounded into space. But whatever vibe he let off it was working, for after a few seconds he realised that the heckling and laughter had died down and the man was coming his way.

The girls were shushing themselves as they saw this beautiful blond, dreaded, muscular fellow slowly making his way towards their little group, towel and shirt in hand.

The girls' lapse into a sudden, deafening silence meant the stranger must be having the same effect on them as he had on Lenox himself. They all admired the sight of the broad-shouldered and lithely toned frame coming in their direction; each muscle in his body working and flexing as he walked bare-footed through the sand. He shook his head once more, his long hair whipping across his face as he shook his dreads free of their watery weight.

Lenox stilled himself as his mind went completely blank, searching for something to say as the reality of the situation hit him hard, sobering him up. He swallowed his nerves as he found himself face-to-face with the man who had been playing on his mind every second of the day since he'd first laid eyes on him.

There was a pause as the man's eyes washed over Lenox, taking in the sight of his taut body through the thin, white, low-cut vest which hugged his full pecs and tight abs perfectly.

"Esperaba verte de nuevo!"

The stranger's voice was equal parts melodic and rough, like the soft, raspy tone of a rock star after a two-hour gig. The Spanish words caught Lenox off guard as they didn't match the way he envisioned them sounding in his head. The accent didn't appear to be local, but it certainly wasn't English.

Through his Cava haze he searched fruitlessly for the meaning of the sentence.

"I'm sorry, what's that?" Lenox asked, deciding he was far too drunk to attempt a Spanish response.

"Oh, apologies," the man responded, placing his hand on his chest in a forgiving gesture "I'm not sure why I assumed you were Spanish. Excuse me."

The girls, as well as Lenox, were silenced by his chivalrousness. They sat there wide-eyed and disbelieving as if they hadn't been convinced that Lenox's vision from this morning actually existed.

"I was just saying I was hoping to see you again."

"Oh," Lenox muttered.

The man quickly held out an iPhone. "I think this belongs to you."

"Oh, my God, my phone. Where did you find it?" Lenox gushed, his face lighting up like a kid at Christmas.

The man laughed at his reaction. "I found it on the beach this morning. When I looked at the home screen I recognised your face in the picture. Took a long shot but was hoping I might run into you here again."

"Oh, my God," he repeated drunkenly. "You are an absolute lifesaver. Thank you so much. I thought it was lost forever!"

"You're welcome. Really. It's my pleasure."

His eyes shone that same aquamarine blue at night that Lenox remembered from their earlier encounter, and again Lenox felt that instant attraction.

There was a brief silence between them as the man's gaze brushed over the unusually quiet girls who were all staring up at him in complete bewilderment from the blanket on the sand.

"Hi!" he offered to them with a shy wave as if he'd just become aware of the gaggle of beautiful girls that surrounded him.

"Oh, I'm sorry. These...are my friends!" Lenox announced with a sweeping gesture of his arm.

When the man responded in his liquid, smoky tone, it was more to Lenox than to the rest of the group. "Hi, I'm Lyric," he said, extending a hand in Lenox's direction.

Lenox paused for a moment too long as the beauty of that word splashed over him. He opened his mouth to speak, but got caught on the utter charm of his name.

Lyric, he repeated to himself in his head, praying that it wasn't out loud.

The sound of Bambi clearing her throat from where she sat removed him from inside his own head.

"Lyric..." He repeated back to him, testing how it felt on his tongue. "I'm Lenox..."

He accepted Lyric's hand and they shook, each taking in the connection and the sensation of their skin touching for the first time.

There was an extended, awkward silence as they continued the languid shaking of the other's hand, their eyes locked on one another's as if they were telling a story with their gaze.

A nervous giggle from one of the girls broke the moment and Lenox could sense movement and shuffling going on behind him. He cleared his own throat before attempting to speak.

"Uh, so do you maybe want to join us for a drink?" he suggested to Lyric, looking behind him with a hopeful glint in his eye which quickly turned to a frown as he noticed his friends beginning to clear up.

"Actually, we might call it a night," Bambi interjected quickly, "but you two stay. There's plenty to drink. Have fun!"

She sounded like an over-protective mother trying to prove to her newly out gay son how cool she was with him hooking up with guys. To Lenox, it came off as less than subtle.

The look in Lenox's eye was intended to let Bambi know that he wasn't quite ready to be alone with his new crush, but she wouldn't have noticed, anyway, as she seemed to be doing everything in her power to avoid his stare altogether.

Lyric let out a stifled laugh of his own as he became aware of what was happening.

"It's okay, if you want to go too, I mean..." Lenox could detect some definite undertones of disappointment to Lyric's words.

"No! I mean I'd love to stay. That is, if you want to..."

Lyric just smiled a sexy sideways grin revealing a row of teeth so white they seemed to gleam in the moonlight.

"Guay!" Lyric responded, which Lenox recognised as translating to "cool" in English.

The girls began to saunter away quietly as if their previous gusto had vanished and they found themselves very self-aware. Bambi was the only one to come and kiss her friend on the cheek before turning to leave.

"It was nice to meet you, Lyric," she added. "You boys have fun…"

As she trotted away after the others, Lenox turned back to Lyric and smiled a tight-lipped smile.

"Can I interest you in a drink?"

"Love one."

Lyric slipped the vest he had been carrying over his head and sat down on the blanket the girls had left behind.

"Is that one of your friends?" Lyric asked before sitting down, his eyes focused on someone down the beach.

"Who?" Lenox followed Lyric's gaze, which was oddly serious. Behind them, a man stood in a strange, erect pose. And although his face was cast in shadow it was clear he was looking towards them.

"No. Don't think so," Lenox said squinting into the darkness. The figure moved, as if he'd been caught out, and turned away from the beach. "That's weird. Anyways. Sit, please!"

Chapter Eight

THEN

Lenox turned back to the situation at hand. He poured Lyric a drink and topped up his own plastic flute at the same time, momentarily allowing himself to get a better look at his new companion.

Beautiful didn't even begin to describe his aura. Lyric was one of those seductively sexy guys who gave off a sense of allure without ever even trying. His dreadlocks were long, neat, and the most amazing shade of soft blond. His skin was the colour of liquid gold which complemented his aqua-hued eyes like sunshine to an afternoon sky. As Lenox handed him his flute, which hummed softly as the carbonated bubbles hit the air, he regarded his inviting features, letting his eyes linger over Lyric's plump lips and soft jaw before resting once again on the fluorescent blue stare that burned into him.

"I love your tattoos," Lenox said as he studied the sleeve of grey and black ink that adorned the entirety of Lyric' right arm. "Are they lotus flowers?"

"Good eye. Do you know the story of how lotus flowers are born?" Lyric asked in his gravelly tone.

Lenox shook his head. Although he knew a little bit about them, he'd rather hear it from those lips.

"A lotus flower begins growing at the bottom of a muddy, murky pool, and slowly emerges towards the surface, bursting out of the water into a beautiful blossom."

Lenox could only stare as he became immersed in the heady beauty of his words.

"Its stem is flexible but does not break. As the lotus flower emerges from the mud and up towards the surface it is completely unstained..."

"That's amazing. I never knew that..."

"It's an incredible flower and such a metaphor for life, don't you think?"

Lenox searched desperately in his mind for something sensible and intelligent to add in the hope of not seeming a complete tool. But he came up empty. Shyly, he looked away.

"What? Don't you agree?"

"I guess...I'm sorry, I've had a little bit too much to drink. I was trying to think of something witty to say. I don't want you to think I'm a ditz or something..."

Lyric stared at him as if mulling over what to say next. He opened his heart-shaped mouth to speak, but seemed to reconsider and took a sip of his drink instead. A moment passed but his eyes never left Lenox. When Lenox looked up he once again was caught in the riptide of his stare, like a boat helplessly lost at sea.

"You've got beautiful eyes..."

Lyric's words caught him off-guard and he smiled back, embarrassed, before tilting his head downwards to study the threads of the blanket.

Lyric reached out a finger underneath Lenox's chin and tipped his head up so they were eye to eye. He paused for a second before drawing Lenox in closer so their lips could touch.

The unexpected kiss was gentle but brimming with feeling. They both closed their eyes and Lenox swam in the sensation of being momentarily connected to Lyric. He felt the heat coming from Lyric's body and his instincts were screaming at him to prolong the kiss further. His tongue wanted to taste the inside of Lyric's mouth and his fingers itched to touch the smooth muscles of his arms.

But as if he had other ideas, Lyric gently pulled away before anything further could happen. His face widened into that same sexy half-smile and he readjusted himself on the blanket before taking another refreshing sip of his drink.

As Lenox smiled back and mimicked his actions, downing most of his Cava in one long haul, his phone started ringing from somewhere on the blanket, the sound muffled from the weight of something pressed on top of it.

Lyric cast his eyes to the direction of the noise. "Looks like you're in high demand tonight," he joked. "So. You here on holiday?" he asked, reminding Lenox he was on earth and changing the subject before he could address his missed call.

"Uh, yes. Sorry. I wasn't expecting that," he gushed, embarrassed by his reddening cheeks.

Lyric flexed the muscles in his jaw as he considered his next thought. "Sorry, I couldn't help myself."

Lenox blushed shyly as he poured himself another half glass and filled Lyric's to the top at the same time.

"Yes. Holiday. You?" he answered almost robotically and took a sip of the fizzy drink.

"No, actually I live here."

"Really? Oh, wow. For how long?"

"Most of my life."

"No way? Really? Were you born here?" Lenox asked with genuine interest. It had always been his dream to live in Ibiza someday. Ever since he knew he wanted to take pictures for a living, he imagined his future as a photographer developing here and thriving among the scenic beauty of the island.

"No, my brother and I were born in the UK but moved here with our parents when we were four."

"Your brother?"

"Twin brother. Identical, actually. Our parents arrived here with the first wave of hippies in the 1960s and never left. After Mum fell pregnant with us she and our dad decided to leave the island for a few years and raise us in their hometown of Brighton, so that we had an idea of where we came from."

"My God, that's amazing. I'm a bit jealous!"

"But, like most who visit the island, it was calling them back and they couldn't resist its magnetic pull. So they brought us back before we started school. And here I am!"

"And your brother and your parents? Are they still here?"

Lyric's eyes suddenly darkened and he looked down at the ground. Lenox waited for him to say something, but it was as if he couldn't find the words.

"Oh, gosh...I'm sorry...Did I...?" He stuttered, trying to come to Lenox's rescue.

"No, it's okay. Sorry. My parents and my brother died, about...I guess it's about ten years ago now..."

Lenox felt both mortified and touched by the vulnerability in Lyric's tone.

"Oh, my God. Oh, Lyric, I'm so sorry. We don't have to talk about this if you don't want to."

"It's fine. Really." He drew in a deep breath as if preparing to launch into something he knew would be difficult. "It was a car accident on the island." He swallowed hard and momentarily averted his gaze from Lenox's. "I wasn't with them..."

Despite Lyric's tough exterior, Lenox could sense that there was still obvious pain behind his eyes.

"Jesus...I can't even imagine. Your twin brother...Were you super close?"

"Inseparable. As you can imagine most identical twins are."

"Oh, Lyric. I can't... I'm so sorry," he repeated, at a loss for something comforting to say.

"His name was Cedar."

"What a beautiful name."

"Unusual, I suppose. Hippy parents."

"Not as unusual as you might think. Take it from someone who has a friend named Bubbles."

They both laughed then. A hearty laugh where their eyes connected and they shared a moment of empathy without having to use any words.

"It's certainly a bit uncommon, but it is Ibiza, after all."

"What was Cedar like?"

Lyric's gaze passed out to the sea as if his memories were stored somewhere on the waves. "Oddly, we weren't that much alike. He was much less of a hippy than I am, quite prim and proper, in truth. But we did everything together..."

Lenox watched as seemed to drift away, like a story was playing itself out behind Lyric's eyes and he was the only one in the audience. Lenox became transfixed, ever the one for a damaged soul, and he waited on tenterhooks for a story that did not come.

There was a hesitation in Lyric's voice followed by an extended silence that verged on awkward as if he wasn't sure if he wanted to continue.

After a minute or two, it became clear to Lenox that was the end of the moment. Lyric straightened up and seemed to refocus his eyes as he cleared his throat, seemingly having returned from wherever he had just been.

"I'm sorry. I'm sharing too much."

"Not at all, really! But if you'd rather not talk about it, I totally understand."

"Thanks. You're quite easy to talk to. I think it does me good to talk about it every now and then. I've been known to keep things bottled up."

Vulnerability looked beautiful on Lyric's features, and Lenox couldn't help but draw some odd sense of pleasure from hearing his story.

"When they passed," Lyric continued, "my parents left me ownership of a number of properties they had acquired on the island."

"Oh, wow! At such a young age?"

"They've been in our family since the early seventies, so they paid next to nothing for them. But because they're so old, most of them need some work."

"Have you ever thought of selling?"

"I've considered it. But to be honest, they're all I have left of my parents. Well, those and the shop. Nowadays, I rent some of them out but mostly I just fluctuate from one to another, depending on the season, since they're quite spread out over the island."

Lenox listened intently to his fluid tones. Lyric's voice oozed laid-back ease which filled him with a sense of subtle relaxation, as if his words were the hands of an experienced masseur. Even the way he sat, with one leg bent in casual fashion at the knee and the other stretched out in front of him, exuded a sense of masculine confidence that Lenox ate up.

"Sounds like a dream come true..."

"I know. I feel lucky every day of my life to be able to call this place home," Lyric said, his eyes casting a net to encompass his surroundings as he spoke. "And of course for what my parents left me..." He paused and returned his gaze to Lenox. "Sorry. Listen to me going on and on."

"No, don't be daft. I'm in awe..."

"In awe?" Lyric repeated back to him.

"Perhaps *envious* would better describe what I'm feeling."

Lyric laughed softly at his remark. "Is this your first time in Ibiza?"

"No, I've been coming here since I was little too."

"Oh, really?"

"Yeah, my parents seem to have fallen in love with the island in the same way yours did, only they never made the move here."

"How come?"

"Not sure. I guess their work was always in the UK. But they loved Ibiza. They started bringing me here as long ago as I can remember. Growing up, I don't honestly remember holidaying anywhere else, in fact."

"They say the island chooses some people, you know."

"I definitely get that. My parents taught me about the history of the land and how to respect it…"

"Sounds like they're quite the connoisseurs."

"I guess you could say that."

There was another pause and the look on Lyric's face told Lenox he was pondering something. His stare was penetrating and the lustful look he gave off sent delicate electric shocks down the route of Lenox's spine. Each time a heavy silence took over between them, Lenox dipped his gaze down to focus on the set of bee-stung lips that wavered just before his own. He could sense his hands begin to tremble as he allowed his mind to explore the fantasy of touching those lips a second time.

But Lyric's words broke the silence once again. "So where do you live, then? Wait. Let me guess. Londoner?"

Lenox paused for a minute, disappointment flooding through him like the air being let out of a balloon.

"Is it that obvious?" he answered, deflated.

"Am I right?" Lyric laughed to himself, opening his mouth wide to reveal his row of perfect teeth.

"Born and raised."

"Lucky guess," he responded sheepishly. "Sorry, I didn't mean to offend…"

"You didn't. Why? Are you not a fan?"

"What? Of London?"

Lenox nodded.

"Yeah, London's cool, I guess…"

The way his voice trailed off gave Lenox an idea of Lyric's true feelings about his hometown.

"But…"

"But, I guess it's not really for me. You know?"

Lenox nodded as they both gazed out at the dark sea laid out in front of them. A moment passed as they sat yet again in silence. Lenox began to fade as the pool of alcohol he had consumed throughout the night swished around inside him.

His thoughts travelled back to the kiss they had shared only instants ago. Short-lived yet rattling at the same time. The longer his mind rested on the sensation of their lips touching, the more his body ached to feel it again. His skin tingled at the thought of feeling Lyric's hands on his body and his mind wandered cheekily to what was hiding inside those figure-hugging board shorts.

The quiet around them was like a heavy fog and Lenox knew that if he didn't act right away the moment would evade him. He drew on his Dutch courage and opened his mouth at the exact moment that Lyric did the same.

They spoke in unison, their words interrupting one another's. They both laughed at the awkwardness of the situation and shyly looked away.

"Sorry. You first," Lyric ventured.

Lenox swallowed again as his empty stomach groaned to be fed something to soak up all the alcohol he had consumed.

"Do you, maybe, if you're up for it..." he stuttered. "Want to go and grab a quick bite?"

Lenox's cheeks grew hot at the awkwardness of his speech. He inwardly castigated himself for acting in such a childish fashion.

Once again, those aquamarine eyes of Lyric's flitted across his face as if he too was being faced with a case of indecisiveness. Every muscle in Lyric's body seemed to flex with his decision-making process.

"That sounds really great..."

Lenox lit up inside despite being able to detect a "but" coming on.

"But, it's getting really late."

There it was.

"And I really should be getting back to the other side of the island."

Lenox's gaze fell to the blanket and he picked at his thumbnail as yet more disappointment weighed him down. There was something about Lyric that made his pulse speed up, like the rush of a wave with an intense energy that surged through him.

"Oh."

It was all Lenox could muster up. He wanted to act cool and aloof as if he was unbothered by this sudden dismissal which sounded like a lame excuse. But instead of the calm and collected response he was rehearsing in his head, paired with a smile and a thank you for joining him, he found himself standing up abruptly and beginning to clear the now empty bottle and plastic glasses away in silence. All the while he avoided eye contact like a stroppy child who was being denied a new toy by his parents.

Lyric stared up at him, seemingly aware that he had struck a nerve and unsure how to rectify it.

"I'm sorry, maybe another time?" Lyric stood as Lenox grabbed the blanket and pulled it away from under him.

"Sure. Whatever. I guess I'll see you around."

But Lenox's words came out less as a question than a short statement devoid of emotion. He was filled with an intense urge to get as far away from the situation as he could. Embarrassment showed in the colour of his cheeks, peppered with rejection, which made for an excruciating cocktail of self-doubt.

"Thanks for the drink..." Lyric tried again.

"Yah, no worries. Have a good night."

And with that, Lenox turned away, blanket in hand, and headed back in the direction of his villa.

As he stumbled carelessly away, he sensed Lyric's gaze studying him from behind and he felt beyond childish for standing up and leaving like he had. But in his mind, it was obvious that Lyric wasn't interested, and from where he was standing, that meant there was no use in sticking around for yet more dismissal.

It didn't matter how childish he felt or looked, anyway. It wasn't as if he was ever going to see him again.

As Lenox struggled to walk drunkenly through the deep sand, his mind couldn't help but begin to reflect on his life now. Perhaps this was what being single again was going to be like. It wasn't as if it was that long since he was on his own the last time. But he certainly didn't expect to be back here so soon. His last relationship, however toxic it had ended up, had given him hope that perhaps he had found someone who really cared for him. He had invested so much energy in making things work, and it wasn't until things got really bad that his friends had opened his eyes to the truth about his abusive boyfriend.

With everything that had happened to Lenox when he was with his ex, he was lucky to have come out of it as unscathed as he was.

Walking towards the road, he heard his phone beep in his pocket. When he pulled it out, the words on the screen caught him off-guard.

Stay away from him.

It was enough to stop him in his tracks as his bleary eyes read and reread the warning emblazoned across his screen, delivered from a blocked number.

He turned back to the beach in a reflex action, suddenly very frightened and hoping that Lyric would still be there so he didn't have to be alone.

But Lyric was gone, and Lenox was surrounded by nothing but darkness as far as the eye could see.

Chapter Nine

Now

"We took the liberty of pulling your file," the female officer stated, rifling through yet even more files from a briefcase on her right before pulling out an envelope with a stamped title that looked all too familiar.

"Numerous acts of criminal behaviour, possession, violence leading to one arrest and one conviction for assault and battery." She paused before lifting her reading glasses to better study his expression. "All before the ripe old age of twelve."

She was trying to rattle him. He'd been down this path before and he knew better than to give anything away without an attorney present. He let her gaze bear down on him, unflinching, returning her penetrating stare with the same conviction. He'd had plenty of practice dealing with authority. People like her didn't bother him anymore. Not since he resigned himself to having nothing left to lose.

"Shall I continue?" she asked, taunting him.

He only needed to gesture as his way of acknowledgement.

"Between the ages of twelve and fifteen, you spent time in and out of a juvenile detention centre. Things seemed to calm down for you then, until you reached seventeen when you were sentenced once again, this time for another count of assault and battery, possession with intent to sell, and the aggravated assault of a police officer."

Her statement came out tinged with doubt as if her records were unclear.

"Are you asking for me to confirm your details, officer? I thought we were just having a trip down memory lane," he retorted with a smirk.

The officer leaned back in her chair and closed her lips tightly before crossing her arms over her chest. He had obviously tapped into something.

"Luckily for you, when you finished your stint in juvie, the court approved a petition and sealed the juvenile records. Therefore, the juvenile court proceedings are treated in many respects as if they never occurred."

"Do you need some water, officer?" he teased, sensing she was out of breath.

"Excuse me?" the male officer began, clearly shocked by his smugness. But he was quickly silenced by his partner's raised hand.

"Oh, I'm just getting started," she continued, unfazed and perhaps a little smug herself. She sat forward again, rifling through more papers. "Just after you turned eighteen...There was an accident. A terrible accident that sent you off the rails. Remember that? Of course, you remember that. How could you not? Because you underwent a psychiatric evaluation and were sentenced to live in an institution, as a patient in the high-security lock-down wing of L'Institut Pere Mata in Reus, Catalonia."

He flinched at the mention of the psychiatric hospital's name; a slight movement that he realised the officers had detected. They exchanged glances before leaning back in their chairs, appearing happy to have finally struck a nerve.

Chapter Ten

THEN

The next morning, Lenox woke up with a hangover that was worse than it should have been, having not drank nearly as much as the pain in his head indicated. He wanted nothing more than to stay in bed and avoid all the nagging stares of his friends. The girls would be sure to accost him downstairs, demanding details of how his night ended with the beautiful dreadlocked stranger from the beach. He wasn't sure he was ready to rehash the rejection and disappointment so soon after the damage to his ego.

Stay away from him.

His whole frame shuddered as if someone had just walked over his grave as he remembered the text he had received on the beach. There was no denying it was odd and somewhat creepy, and certainly threatened to prey on Lenox's overactive and paranoid imagination, but it wasn't the first time Lenox had received a text warning him to back off from whatever conquest he was after. He made a conscious decision to push it to the back of his mind and get back to enjoying his holiday. Sexless as it was sure to be.

He attempted to turn over and go back to sleep but the unforgiving Ibizan sun was already high in the sky and demanding attention. As Lenox lay there in his king-sized bed, he could already detect its heat. Moments later, he succumbed to its demands and lazily pulled back the sheet and dragged himself out of bed.

When he spied the clock on the wall, he realised it was much later than he'd thought. He prepared himself for the onslaught that was sure to hit when he reached the kitchen, but to his surprise he was greeted with nothing but silence. The house appeared empty and tidy, the only giveaway to the recently departed presence of others the sharp scent of freshly brewed coffee coming from the percolator on the counter.

As he poured himself a generous mug of black coffee, he saw the note which lay on the counter. It was written in Bambi's familiar, loopy script.

Hey sleepyhead,

We're at the beach. Take your time. Hope you had fun last night, stud!

Can't wait to hear all the raunchy details,
B

Lenox groaned as he took a deep sip of the bitter drink. He paused with his eyes closed to feel the full effect on his core as the caffeine did what it was intended to do.

After a moment's reflection, Lenox decided that he wasn't going to do his usual "feel sorry for me" song and dance. He was on holiday and, after a year's worth of bloody hard work at university, he was damn well going to enjoy his time on the island, regardless of last night's slight setback to his ego.

He finished his drink, took a quick shower, and set off for the beach.

The air outside was hot and sticky and the sun beat down on him with a fiery intensity that instantly slowed his pace and almost took his breath away. As he wandered in the direction of the water he allowed himself to take in the scenery around him. Casting his lucid gazed over the surrounding palm trees and turquoise hue to the sea, he felt a million miles from in the stresses of London. This was his time to relax and unwind and let go of all the pressing and demanding aspects of his life back in the UK. Here, he could get back to himself and not fuss or worry about anything.

It wasn't difficult to spot his vagabond crew from where they perched by the water's edge. It was hard for them not to command attention when they went out together. And this morning was no exception. Tulip, Del Rey, and Bubbles were all topless, which was no surprise; the only thing that hid their modesty was the tiniest slip of fabric, practically flossing the skin between their legs. Bambi wore a bikini top. Although not at all ashamed of her 32 C breasts, she preferred to keep some things to the imagination outside the walls of the strip club.

The girls were sprawled out on colourful beach towels like an ad for tanning lotion, their bodies glistening sleek and bronzed beneath the shimmering rays of the sun.

Tulip was the first to spot Lenox as he approached. He peeled off his navy-blue vest and spread his towel out in a position that best optimised the current position of the sun.

"Morning, sunshine," she joshed, her wide red lips spreading into a mischievous grin. "Good of you to join us."

"Finally," Del Rey added.

"We've been here for ages, why'd you sleep so late?" Bubbles chimed in.

"He's late because he had a *wild* night last night," Bambi interjected, not waiting for Lenox to respond on his own.

"Well I hate to disappoint..." He grabbed Bambi's Hawaiian Tropic dry-oil spray and slathered his skin.

"Oh, don't you even say it, Mister Winter. That guy was practically handed to you on a silver freakin' platter," Bambi tutted, removing her oversized Jackie O sunglasses so he could get the full effect of her disapproving and disappointed stare.

"Hey, no one was more disappointed than I. And believe you me, I tried!"

"You tried, did ya?"

"Harder than I did in my year twelve law exam..." Lenox quipped.

"What happened?" Tulip asked with genuine concern.

Lenox sighed and rested back on his elbows, feeling the searing heat on his skin already.

"I dunno." He shrugged. "I guess he just wasn't into me."

The girls exchanged an all-knowing glance with one another which Lenox clocked, sitting up at attention now.

"What?"

Bubbles giggled as the tension rose.

"Did I miss something?"

"Well, if he wasn't into you, he sure must have a lot of time on his hands because he's been sitting over there waiting for you for the last hour..."

Bambi tilted her chin in the direction behind where Lenox sat. Following her gaze, it took him a second to put together what she was signalling.

Perched on a beach lounger, in that same exact way as the first time he saw him, was Lyric. Lenox's heart picked up speed as excitement began to prickle at his scalp.

Lyric had his eyes cast down at the guitar in his hands and he seemed to be engrossed in the strings he was picking. His full lips were pursed as if they were hugging the words to a song Lenox couldn't hear, and his brow was furrowed ever so slightly with the emotion of the melody he strummed. His muscular tanned legs were stretched out in front of him in that same casual manner that sent the blood rushing between Lenox's legs, and his bare chest made Lenox wonder if he actually owned a shirt.

The sound of the gentle waves seemed to quiet down and Lenox imagined the song Lyric was playing. He could almost feel the words as they wrapped themselves warmly around him like a cashmere blanket.

After a moment, lost in a fantasy that only he was a part of, Lyric looked up from his guitar and caught Lenox's stare. He held it for a moment as he continued to play like he was composing a song that was just for Lenox. He smiled and Lenox felt instantly at ease. He returned the smile then forced himself to look away and back to his friends who he had almost forgotten about.

"Holy shit!" he mumbled, very thirsty all of a sudden. "He's over there."

"We know," Del Rey said curtly.

"What is he doing here?" Lenox continued as nerves took over.

"He's waiting for you, obviously." Bambi cut in. "He came over as soon as we got here, asking if you were with us."

"Really?" Lenox was incredulous.

"Yes, really!" Bambi replied. "So I don't know what you believe happened last night through your champagne haze, but you obviously didn't strike out as much as you think you did, otherwise he wouldn't have come down here looking for you."

Lenox looked down at the sand, gathering his thoughts. Bambi was right. Maybe it hadn't gone as badly as he remembered. Perhaps he still had a chance.

A chance at *what,* he wasn't sure.

"What are you waiting for?" Tulip whispered.

"What?"

"Go over there!"

Lenox nodded and took a deep breath. As he slowly approached where Lyric sat he gave him a shy wave and instantly regretted it, feeling juvenile and unsure of himself.

Lyric didn't take much notice. Instead, he put down his guitar and sat up with his bare feet in the sand. He was the first to speak.

"*Buenos días*," he said in that raspy tone that Lenox had prayed he'd get the chance to appreciate again.

"Good morning," Lenox responded in English.

"Your friends said you'd be along soon enough."

"Have you really been waiting here for *me?*"

Lyric just nodded, squinting up at him through the harsh light of the sun. He padded the seat next to him, inviting Lenox to sit.

"How are you?" Lenox asked, accepting the invitation.

"I'm good, thanks. How are you feeling?"

Lenox nodded, understanding the subtle dig at how drunk he was last night. "Yeah, feeling all right. I guess." He leaned forward, resting his forearms on his thighs, and steepled his hands. "Look, I'm sorry for last night..."

"Sorry for what?"

"Sorry for shooting off in a bit of a huff..."

Lyric stared, sensing he wasn't finished.

"I guess I had a bit too much to drink."

"No worries, I'm glad I got to see you again."

"You are?"

"Sure! Why wouldn't I be?"

"Well, I thought...I guess I just assumed when you didn't want to..."

"You mean get a bite to eat?"

"Well, yeah..."

Lyric leaned in, closing the distance between them a bit. He reached out a finger and pulled Lenox's face towards his own until they were once again eye to eye. Lenox found himself drowning in those fluorescent blue eyes and felt the world around him begin to slow to a stop.

"I just didn't want to do something I'd regret and that you wouldn't remember."

"Something you'd regret?" Lenox repeated his words back to him.

"Well, less that I'd regret, and more that you wouldn't remember enough to appreciate..."

And with that, Lyric pulled his face in for a kiss, planting his lusciously full lips on Lenox's mouth. Memories of last night's embrace came flooding back to Lenox like still frames from a film. He closed his eyes and let himself fall deep into the kiss; Lyric's pillowy soft mouth pressing up against his own, firm yet gentle, sweet yet lustful.

Lenox waited for him to pull away like the last time, only he didn't. Instead he pulled himself in closer, hungrier, as if he couldn't get enough of Lenox's taste. Lenox met his intensity and returned it with the same gusto; a slave to his instinct and unaware of rational thought.

Their lips parted and Lyric pushed his tongue into Lenox's mouth. It was warm and wet and searching, and Lenox's body reacted to the sensation of having a part of Lyric inside his body. He found Lyric's face with his hands and gently traced the line of his jaw from his chin to the back of his head until he reached the mane of thick dreadlocks which cascaded down Lyric's back. Lyric returned the gesture and let his own hands find Lenox's face, his fingertips dancing gently across his stubbled cheeks and tangling themselves in his long black hair.

His hands were strong as they pulled Lenox's face in closer. Their noses touched and their heads tilted to opposite sides to make room for their kiss. Lenox was enslaved to his passion and shifted his body to make room for his hardening cock inside his shorts. The creak of the beach lounger beneath him reminded him of where he was and he quickly pulled away from their embrace.

Licking his lips, he looked away, struck with worry as to the scene they'd probably caused on the beach.

"I'm sorry...I'm not usually so..."

"Don't be," Lyric interrupted, casting a glance around him. "Take a look. I don't think anyone even blinked an eye!"

Lenox looked around him and saw that he was right. No one seemed to notice the two of them.

"This is Ibiza, after all," Lyric added, sitting back and adopting a casual pose, one knee bent and tucked up underneath him on the chair.

Lenox turned to face him, unable to wipe the grin from his face.

"Listen, I don't want to keep you from your friends, but I was wondering..." He paused, baiting Lenox with his inviting tone. "Do you have any plans for dinner tonight?"

"Tonight?" he repeated, stealing a glance back towards his friends.

"Because I'd love to take *you* out for that bite."

"That would be...Great."

"Excellent. Shall I pick you up?"

"Yes, sounds perfect."

Lenox tapped the address of the villa they were staying at and his own phone number into Lyric's mobile. Lyric picked up his guitar and strode confidently away down the beach. Even the way he moved, his perky round arse swaying gently from side to side as he walked, had a hypnotising effect on Lenox. It wasn't until he had disappeared behind a corner that Lenox was able to look away. When he turned back to his female entourage, the looks on their astonished faces said it all.

Chapter Eleven

THEN

Lyric owned a Jeep Wrangler 4 X 4. In typical Ibizan style, although painted white, it appeared more of a deep grey due to the thick layer of dust that covered every inch. The seats were worn yet comfortable, and as Lenox climbed into the passenger side he felt like he was at the helm of a safari vehicle.

Lenox had been anticipating this moment all afternoon and now he was finally back, sitting side by side with this gorgeous man he couldn't get out of his head and whose taste he'd had on his lips since this morning, he was almost vibrating with nervous excitement. Bambi had helped him choose an appropriate outfit that said casual yet up for anything. They had settled with an oversized white vest and black distressed denim shorts.

Lyric was dressed in a smart deep blue short-sleeved button-down shirt and sandblasted denim shorts. He smelled a deliciously masculine and fresh combination of vanilla and mint. His golden skin radiated heat and Lenox swore the intense hue of his eyes could act as a torch in the night sky. He tossed a few dreadlocks off his shoulder and leaned in to kiss Lenox gently and traditionally on the left cheek then the right. Although it wasn't where he was hoping to be kissed, Lenox accepted it shyly and flashed a toothy smile back at him.

"Hi," Lyric breathed, returning his smile with a lazy grin.

"How are you?" Lenox asked, breathing deeply and desperately trying to rid himself of his nervous twitches.

"All right, thanks. Hungry?" He put the Jeep into gear and set off down the narrow road.

Lyric took him to a magnificent restaurant called Teatro Pereyra, set in a beautiful old building in Ibiza Old Town. It had high ceilings and once had a cinema at the back. As they were ushered to a quaint, very private table for two off to the side, Lenox noticed the tall, red velvet curtains that remained from when it had served as a theatre.

A slinky waitress with a high, glossy ponytail was at their side to take their drink order even before they sat down. Lyric spoke to her in Spanish and they exchanged some pleasantries before he turned to Lenox and asked, "Red?"

"Excellent!" he answered, confirming his taste in wine.

The waitress glided off after flashing them both a warm smile and uttering something that Lenox couldn't understand.

"This place is amazing," he ventured, looking around once more at the understated lavishness of the place.

"I love it here. They have a strict, how do you say, anti-VIP rule to keep it separate from the overwhelming commercialism of the island."

"Oh, really?"

"Yeah, when the island became popular with the club scene in the eighties, so many local businesses suffered from the booming tourism and the high demand for posh restaurants and lounges. But this place remains untouched. It's incredible on the weekends when they hold live music nights."

"Wow, sounds authentic."

"It's been around since 1889."

Lenox was in awe of Lyric's apparent wealth of knowledge about his beautiful home, and his seductively rounded English-Spanish accent only accentuated his allure even further.

The waitress returned with their wine and two tall, thin-stemmed glasses that sparkled in the candlelight. She proudly displayed the label to them as though she was showing off a new car before corking the bottle and pouring a modest amount of wine in each of their glasses.

Lyric held up his glass and looked Lenox in the eye.

"What shall we toast to?" he asked, nailing him with another stirring smile.

"To...Hot summer nights..."

Lyric grinned madly in his direction before adding, "And even *hotter* company."

As they clinked glasses, Lenox was thankful for the dim lighting that surely masked his blushing cheeks.

THEIR CONVERSATION FLOWED as easily as the wine as they dined on an incredible variety of tapas. A solo guitarist strummed an acoustic tune on the small stage behind them as they ate and drank and talked, sharing tales of friendships and family.

Lenox was amazed to hear that Lyric worked in a modest café on the Northern part of the island that he owned; gifted to him from his parents. He managed a staff of three and made his own hours that often changed depending on the volume of business and the time of year. His life seemed beautifully simplistic; a far cry from the hustle and stress and noise of London that was Lenox's world, and Lenox found himself filled with a gentle feeling of envy for the life that Lyric had built for himself here in paradise.

"So, you're a photographer?" Lyric said.

"Well, I hope to be. One day."

"Do you have any of your pictures on your phone?"

Lenox hesitated, ever the modest one. "Well, a couple...I guess."

"Can I see a few?"

"I dunno..."

"Oh, come on, please? I bet they're amazing."

Lenox caved and pulled out his phone. He unlocked the screen and swiped through his pictures, trying to find an album that would showcase his talent and not make him appear to be some sort of pretentious poser as he feared they might.

"Oh, God, these are all so...Wait, here's a couple nice ones."

He tilted the screen so Lyric could get a good look and he swiped right through a series he had taken on wild flowers.

"Oh, wow, these are beautiful."

"I've always loved flowers. My mother used to fill our house with them growing up. Every room would have a vase brimming with the most beautiful and overlooked blooms, every colour you could imagine. I suppose that's where I get my appreciation from."

"You know, if we could see the miracle of a single flower clearly, our whole life would change."

Lyric's words were like poetry and struck a chord with Lenox somewhere deep inside his stomach. He stopped flicking the pictures and stared at Lyric who seemed even more stunning and beautiful than he had only an instant before. Lyric, sensing his eyes on him, turned away from the phone and met his stare. They shared a silence for a moment, their bodies still and their breathing slowed, before Lyric broke the trance and spoke.

"You wanna get outta here?"

Chapter Twelve

THEN

Lyric brought them back to one of his parents' many properties, only a short walk from where they had had dinner. That was lucky considering how much wine they had both drunk, which would have made it difficult to drive.

It was a modest flat, high up in the D'Alt Villa and down a little alley that Lenox was sure he wouldn't have even known was there in the light of day. They stumbled through the doorway and into the narrow front hall, giggling and touching each other nonchalantly like it was the most natural thing in the world. There was no denying why Lyric had brought him there. Yet Lenox carried on the charade of pretending he was interested in the decor and architecture of the apartment before the moment came when it was acceptable to let go.

They made it into the front room, Lyric holding Lenox by the hand and pulling him along until they were side by side and facing the sectional sofa that took up most of the south wall of the lounge. Lenox was caught off-guard by the incredible view through the huge floor-to-ceiling picture windows that opened out onto the illuminated city below.

"Oh, wow," he breathed, dropping Lyric's hand and taking a step closer to the window to get a better look. "You can see everything from up here."

"Will you excuse me for a moment?" Lyric asked.

Lenox nodded as Lyric disappeared into another room, and turned back to the view. He breathed in deeply, taking in the moment and being as present in the now as he could. This was exactly what he needed. Distraction and good company. Lyric was beautiful, intelligent, and sensitive. Exactly the type that Lenox knew he should always go for. Unfortunately, his head sometimes led himself in another direction and he ended up with much less desirable company.

His phone rang from inside his pocket. He considered not even checking to see who it was, but curiosity got the better of him. He was surprised to see BLOCKED come up on the caller ID. He ignored the call and cast his eyes over the city once more.

A moment later, he sensed Lyric approaching him from behind and he allowed himself to close his eyes and breathe in the scent of his body. Lyric's breath was warm on his bare neck. When he opened his eyes, Lyric's face, full of a lustful intensity, was reflected in the glass before Lyric wrapped his firm hands around his waist and pulled him in closer.

Lenox moaned at the sudden change in sensation of Lyric's body against his own.

"Mmm, you smell different. What is that? Vanilla?"

But Lyric didn't answer. Lenox pressed his hands on the glass of the window as Lyric's lips delicately brushed the bare skin from his earlobe to his shoulder, leaving the area quivering and aching for more. Behind him, Lyric stiffened in his shorts as he pushed his hands up inside Lenox's vest, exploring the skin of his chest and abs before slipping inside the waistband of his Calvin Kleins.

"Oh, fuck," Lenox whispered as his shorts tightened around his growing erection.

"I want you so badly," Lyric muttered back between gentle suckling kisses he was placing on Lenox's neck. His voice was different. Carnal almost. And his touch was slightly rougher.

Those words were enough to make Lenox explode right there on the spot. He spun himself around so they were face-to-face and Lenox's back was now pressed up against the glass. He looked Lyric in the eye, pausing briefly as he noticed that their normal bright blue tint seemed darker somehow, almost brownish, before peeling his white vest over his head and letting it fall to the floor around him.

Lyric's gaze fell to Lenox's muscular bare chest. Immediately he began unbuttoning his own shirt. He pulled it over his broad shoulders and discarded it behind him. Their hands were on each other like bees on a flower, rubbing and sensing and grasping. They kissed feverishly as they each reached to undo their belts and shorts. To pull his mouth from Lyric's for even a moment was torturous to Lenox, like a piece of his own body had been ripped away. Their mouths fit together so perfectly, like two lost pieces of a jigsaw puzzle, and as they wrapped their arms around each other, shorts half-unzipped and hanging off their hips, the feeling of Lyric's erect nipples grazing against his sent ripples of dreamy pleasure through him.

Lyric pulled away and began his descent of Lenox's body, his hands playing with Lenox's nipples as his tongue traced the lines of his smooth chest. Lenox twisted and tugged at Lyric's dreadlocks as Lyric's head moved slowly to his abs, licking and kissing his washboard stomach. He groaned with pleasure as Lyric found the zipper of his shorts and pulled it down.

Lenox's hard cock was throbbing and practically begging to be released from the confines of his turquoise AussieBum briefs. Lyric kissed it gently through the soft Spandex of his underwear before tugging at the elastic waistband and commencing the slow reveal. His lips kissed the treasure trail of soft dark hairs that travelled south from Lenox's navel to his dick. Lenox tensed as his modesty was revealed and Lyric stood back for a second to marvel at the size of his cock. He reached around and massaged Lenox's arse cheeks, locating his arsehole and touching it. Then he took his penis in both hands, one at the base and one towards the tip, and eased its glistening head into his mouth.

Lenox let out a raspy moan from deep in his belly as he let go and revelled in the sensation of having his cock sucked so deliciously. Lyric took his time, sucking long and hard; his mouth moving up and down the length of his shaft until his lips just grazed the pubic hairs at the base, deep-throating Lenox as much as he could. Lenox arched his back, letting go of Lyric's head and twining his hands in his own hair. He tugged at his black locks as his bare back pressed up against the glass, giving those down on the street a show they hadn't anticipated. He played with his own nipples for a moment, stroking his pecs and adding to the ecstasy of the blow job he was receiving. Up and down Lyric's head travelled. He swallowed Lenox's pre-come with increasing intensity as Lenox's frame began to buck.

Lenox was too lost in the sensation to stop him. Another few moments of this momentum and he surely would have lost it. Lyric paused, sensing he was close, and glanced up to study him. Lenox looked down and pulled him to his feet so that they were once again face-to-face. He kissed his lips, licking the sticky juices from Lyric's mouth.

Lyric offered the most gorgeous smile, brimming with excitement over what was to come. He took Lenox by the hand and led him into a bedroom across the lounge.

"I think the people below us have had enough of a free show." He mirrored Lenox's thoughts perfectly.

Lenox shook with the building intensity of his inevitable orgasm and he tried to still himself, knowing the best was yet to come.

When they got into the bedroom, Lyric dropped his hand, leaving him at the foot of the bed and illuminating the room by switching on a small side lamp which cast a pleasant, ambient glow on the walls. He made eye contact with Lenox as he pulled a small, square foil packet from his back pocket before letting his shorts fall to his feet. He stepped out of them, and it was Lenox's turn to gawk at the size of what Lyric had been hiding in his own trousers. From the imprint it made in his underwear as it stretched the material of his pink briefs, Lenox could tell he had a massive package.

Lyric strode confidently over to him before easing his own underwear down, his long, thick cock springing back against his pubic region as it was released. Lenox could feel his mouth open into an "o" shape as he took in the sight of Lyric fully naked.

When he lifted his eyes, Lyric kissed him sweetly; much softer than before yet with more intensity behind it. He pulled back and looked Lenox square in the eye, his chin trembling slightly.

"I want you to make love to me."

Lenox was turned on by his choice of words and took the condom that was passed to him. Without breaking their eye contact, Lyric lowered himself down onto the bed. He spread his legs wide and invited Lenox to climb on top.

Lenox unwrapped the condom, slid it over his cock, and climbed onto the bed, fitting himself in-between Lyric's strong, golden-haired legs. He tugged on Lyric's cock, pleasuring him as his own dick adjusted itself so that it was pressing up against Lyric's arsehole. Lyric closed his eyes as Lenox jerked him off slowly and began pushing the head of his penis inside him.

It took a moment for both of their bodies to adjust and relax as Lenox began to insert himself fully inside. Lyric tensed for a moment as his arse opened up and relaxed to make way for Lenox's girth.

"You okay?" Lenox breathed, stilling himself as Lyric arched his back and head, tilting his chin to the ceiling. Lenox kissed his neck softly as Lyric took deep breaths, making space in his body.

"Go slow...Please?" he pleaded although he had to know Lenox would.

Lenox nodded and furrowed his brow as he pushed himself in further. They both moaned in excruciating pleasure as their bodies joined together as one. Lyric wrapped his strong legs around Lenox's lower body, relaxing further and allowing Lenox to go deeper inside. When he inserted his whole length, Lenox paused and once again found Lyric's lips, his tongue entering his mouth. They kissed passionately as instinct took over and Lenox began to thrust his hips.

Lyric cried out as Lenox fucked him, slow and deep. His cock moved in and out like the tides of the ocean. Each thrust increased in speed until they were like the cogs in a well-greased machine, moving without a hitch, faster and faster. As they gained momentum, Lenox reached down and found Lyric's cock and mimicked the speed and intensity of his thrusts.

Lenox ground his teeth together as he fucked Lyric, sucking in air through a clenched jaw. Lyric reached behind his head and grabbed hold of the headboard, tensing his biceps as he pulled. Lenox took in the sight of this gorgeous man beneath him, muscles flexed and jaw tight. Perspiration was forming on their bodies, creating a sweaty film between them. They cried out in unison as their orgasms moved closer and closer to the surface. Lenox thrust in and out, his sweaty cock pumping away furiously at Lyric's ass.

Just as they were about to tip over the edge, Lyric let go of the headboard and dug his nails into Lenox's back, causing him to call out as pleasure mixed with pain and took hold of his nervous system.

"Make love to me, come for me," Lyric moaned. Their bodies bucked as they both tipped over and orgasmed.

They came together, over and over. Each thrust of Lenox's cock sent wave after wave of come up inside Lyric, who exploded in Lenox's hand. A sticky, cloudy mess of semen coated his palm as it worked the head of Lyric's dick, stroking it up and down until every last drop had been expelled.

As Lenox's hips began to slow, Lyric caught him off guard by taking charge and flipping them both over suddenly, with Lenox still hard and fully inserted inside Lyric. Once on top, Lyric lifted himself off Lenox and once again sunk his head to Lenox's hips. Ripping off the condom, he bent and wrapped his full lips around Lenox's girth once more.

The sensation of having a hot mouth around his dick after coming only moments before was like nothing he had ever experienced. Lenox arched his back and cried out in surprise and pure ecstasy as Lyric sucked the engorged mushroom head of his member until there was nothing left.

When he was finished, and their breath had finally returned, Lyric looked into Lenox's eyes; a lazy and satiated expression played across his face. Lenox smiled down at him. A smile that spoke his happiness and fulfilment without uttering a word. Lyric returned his happy gaze and lowered himself onto the mattress beside him, so that their slick bodies touched but both were looking up at the ceiling.

Exhaustion stilled them both as lazy smiles morphed into dozy grins. The gentle hum of people on the streets below was like a lullaby, drifting them off into unconsciousness. A cool breeze blew through an open window somewhere and licked at their sweaty bodies as they sunk deeper into sleep.

Lenox was filled with a sense of utter content. He would sleep well tonight, next to this beautiful man, cocooned in this beautiful apartment, high above the streets and nestled in the rolling hills.

He wasn't sure what time it was as he lay there, moments from sleep, and he didn't really care. But just before he closed his eyes completely and drifted into blissful unawareness, he thought he'd better check his phone in case anybody was looking for him. As the screen came to life with the touch of the home key, it was blank.

He had half-expected to see another creepy text, and was relieved by the lack of one. He hadn't told the girls. Their reaction would only have added to his growing paranoia and that was the last thing he needed. He hadn't a clue who could have sent the earlier message to him, but he wasn't going to let his mind run away with him and he resolved to try to forget about it. He replaced the phone on the bedside table, face down, and rolled over to sleep.

Chapter Thirteen

THEN

When Lenox opened his eyes the next morning, he had one of those moments where he was unsure as to where he was. Sunlight drifted in through an open window to his left, with long, sheer floor-to-ceiling curtains billowing in the early morning breeze, and he was brought back to the night before when he'd first glanced out of that same window at the busy streets below.

His mind swept back to the blocked call he'd received. Lenox had cleared it from his phone as if the motion of deleting the alert would wipe it from his subconscious. But as he lay there in bed the morning after, the memory was stronger than before. He had fired off a quick text to Bambi, to check that it wasn't her or one of the other girls calling. But she had assured him that they were all fine and that he should enjoy his evening, leaving him to drift off into an interrupted sleep. He drew in a deep breath and tried to push the nagging worry down into the pit of his stomach.

Turning over in the bed, he was surprised to see an empty spot next to him where he was hoping Lyric would be. The bed felt cold and unfamiliar and he was struck with a fleeting sensation that he had been ditched by his date.

But the sounds coming from somewhere else in the apartment indicated otherwise, and Lenox tossed back the crisp white sheets and padded towards the noise. To his delight, he was greeted with the sight of Lyric, naked except for his Calvin Klein briefs, cooking something delicious-smelling in the kitchen.

When Lyric spotted Lenox, he flashed him the most inviting, toothy smile and immediately stopped what he was doing to greet him.

"*Buenos días*," he chirped, planting a sweet kiss on Lenox's lips.

"Good morning," Lenox answered bashfully as the butterflies in his stomach resumed their frantic fluttering. He noticed that the bright blueness to Lyric's eyes had returned and the vanilla scent to his skin he'd noticed last night had dissipated.

"I hope you're hungry. French toast?" Lyric stirred a concoction in the frying pan.

"Smells amazing."

"It's my mother's recipe. She was well-known for whipping it up in the café when she was still working there. I've been told mine's not too bad, although nothing compared to hers."

"I'm sure you're being modest..."

"Well, I'll let you be the judge. Freshly squeezed orange juice?"

"That would be amazing."

Lenox moved to a kitchen stool that was placed by the island on which Lyric was busy preparing breakfast. For a moment, he allowed his eyes to feast on the sight of Lyric's muscular frame, mixing and pouring. Lyric's blond dreads were scooped up off his face and twirled into a bun on top of his head, showing off his sculpted jaw and strong cheekbones. As he worked, his biceps flexed with each movement of his arms, sending little waves of subtle pleasure to Lenox's groin.

Lyric caught him staring, resting his chin in his hand as he drank in the sight of a beautiful man making him breakfast, and his face erupted into a wide-mouthed grin.

"Sleep well?" he asked, transferring the mixture from the bowl to a frying pan.

"Mmm," Lenox mumbled, not wanting to bring up the text from the other night or the missed call. "It was surprisingly quiet, despite being so close to the town centre."

"Yeah, the acoustics up here are pretty amazing. It's what drew my parents to the property in the first place. They wanted somewhere that was near to the hustle and flow but high up enough to be still at night. Here, try this..." Lyric dipped two fingers elegantly into the mixture and invited Lenox to taste.

Lenox opened his mouth and sucked the sweet mixture off his hand, eyes locked on Lyric as the stirring inside his underwear grew stronger with the intensely erotic gesture. He let his tongue linger as it licked off the batter from around Lyric's fingers, before slowly pulling back and licking the residue from his lips. He seemed to have achieved the desired effect as Lyric's eyes grew darker and he tilted his chin down and took deep breaths, his frame rising and contracting as little chills made him quiver. Lenox's gaze wavered for a moment as he judged the quickest way back to the bedroom from where he sat. Lyric followed his gaze, adrenaline building between them as a decision seemed to flash across his features.

"Fuck it," Lyric breathed as he pushed all the dishes and bowls to one side, clearing a space on the worktop and sending plastic and glass crashing to the floor.

Lenox reacted in surprise for only a moment before returning to Lyric. As if reading each other's thoughts, they both sprang into action, lips connecting in an implosion of passion. They groped and massaged one another's bare skin as Lyric climbed up on top of the granite worktop that separated them, knees spreading so he could lean down and kiss Lenox. Their mouths moved as one, tongues licking and sucking as he knotted his hands in Lenox's loose black hair, pulling his head in closer to experience as much of him as he could.

Lenox placed his hands on Lyric's thighs, drawing him in closer until Lyric sat fully on the counter, bare feet dangling over the side. He straddled Lenox, who had stood up from his chair. Lenox grabbed him by the arse and scooted him closer to the edge on which he sat so that they were pressed up against one another, pelvis to pelvis.

Lyric's head fell back to look at the ceiling as Lenox's lips moved down his neck. Lenox grasped at his pecs and tweaked his round, dark nipples. His tongue followed and licked and sucked the smooth skin of his chest. Lyric leaned back so his elbows were resting on the cold, hard counter and spread his legs wider, obviously hoping that Lenox would continue his erotic descent on his body.

Their breathing was short and quick as adrenaline and passion tainted their bodies red, their flesh hot and sensitive to touch and perspiration already beginning to bead on their bodies.

Lyric was hard as a rock already as Lenox brushed his hand over the material of his briefs teasingly and his tongue traced the defined grooves of his six-pack.

"Oh, fuck, I want you so badly," Lyric muttered, his head tossed back and almost flat against the counter. His back arched as Lenox peeled back the waistband of his briefs, letting his erect cock spring up.

Lenox looked at him for only a moment and watched Lyric's expression as he peered down, anticipating the delicious pleasure that was to come. Then he sunk his head down and took Lyric into his mouth.

The feeling of having Lyric's cock in his mouth was divine and as he worked it between his lips, he sensed Lyric sit, presumably to get a better look. Lenox worked away at his dick, his head rising and dipping in long, perfect strokes as he licked and sucked with increasing intensity.

Lenox sensed Lyric's frame begin to stiffen further as he moved closer and closer to the breaking point. Lyric's hands were in his hair once more, cupping his head and rising and falling with the movement of his mouth. Lenox paused for a moment, before gripping Lyric's length and jerking it up and down as Lyric strained his neck, reaching up to kiss him. Lyric moaned his appreciation and approval as he tasted his own juices which coated Lenox's lips. They kissed hungrily for a second as Lenox pulled his briefs down over the curve of his perky arse. He kicked them to the side and stroked his cock which was now erect and shuddering as it pierced the air with its stiffness.

"You're so good at that," Lyric said between their feverish kisses.

Lyric scooted off the countertop so that they were eye to eye and each stroking their own throbbing cock as they climbed closer and closer to ecstasy.

"You taste so good," Lenox murmured back. He reached his free hand around and grabbed Lyric's arse now that it was level with his own. Lyric groaned at the sensation as Lenox moved his searching fingers and found his hole, circling and prodding it gently.

"Oh, *Jesus,*" Lyric gasped as Lenox's finger entered him.

"Come for me, baby," Lenox whispered, his lips next to Lyric's ear as his finger moved in and out of his arse.

"I'm coming, I'm fucking coming."

"Oh, God, yes, I'm coming too."

They came together—an exquisite release that rocked their cores and caused them to call out as their bodies bucked and shook. Lenox orgasmed so intensely he could almost see stars behind his closed eyelids. Lyric's fingertips dug into Lenox's skin as the last waves of his ejaculation ravaged through him. It was a moment of beautiful unity.

When they finally opened their eyes, a smile spread across Lenox's face as Lyric took in the mess around them.

"Let's go out for breakfast."

Chapter Fourteen

T̲HEN

Lyric took them to his café, which was a twenty-minute ride out of the old town. They passed through a quaint village called San Joan on a very winding road before arriving at Cala San Vicente, a somewhat touristy but tucked-away little spot where the café, On the Beach, was perched behind a row of incredibly tall bamboo trees.

Inside, it was decorated like a kitschy old-fashioned Tiki bar, with surfboards and other beach paraphernalia adorning the walls and ceiling. Enormous Buddhas sat in corners surrounded by uplifting quotes carved into driftwood that hung from all areas. It was colourful and fun and made Lenox pause as he entered, his eyes dancing over the decor and taking it all in. It seemed as if every inch of the place had something hanging from it, with no beam left unadorned.

It was early and the café was not open for business yet. Lyric locked the door behind him and walked over to the bar area and began making coffee as Lenox continued his exploration.

"What do you think?" Lyric asked, busying himself with opening a new bag of Ibiza blend ground coffee he found on a shelf.

"It's amazing," he said, skirting the outer walls. "Is this all you? I mean, did you decorate it like this?"

Lyric nodded as he turned around for a moment, basking in Lenox's appreciation. "I didn't want it to look like it was taking itself too seriously. Hence the combination of beach junk and Asian-inspired art."

Lenox returned his gaze to where Lyric stood behind the bar. "I love it."

And the truth was, he did. He loved how much Lyric was not like the guys he hooked up with in London. Lyric wasn't afraid to be himself and, like his café, knew not to take himself or life too seriously. He had a *joie de vivre* that was reflected in his appearance, as well as the way he lived his life. There was nothing about him that seemed fake or forced, and it made Lenox feel like he could really be himself around him. He didn't have to put on an act, or pretend to like something he didn't or even put up with any annoying habits or traits.

It had only been a couple of days since they had first laid eyes on each other, but Lenox could already feel himself begin to *sway* a bit with Lyric—a word he and Bambi used to describe when they really clicked with someone.

He perched on a barstool and watched Lyric move gracefully behind the counter, emanating ease and self-assuredness. His stomach fluttered and flipped as his true feelings started coming to the surface.

Lenox and Lyric finally sat down at a table for two that overlooked the beautiful sandy beach with the most incredible turquoise waters that Lenox had ever seen. The food was well worth the wait. Lyric's French toast was sumptuous and filled the gap in Lenox's stomach that had begun to groan and moan since they'd had sex earlier.

"So, tell me about your life back in the UK."

"What do you want to know?"

Lyric finished his bite of French toast and took a long haul on his tall glass of orange juice before answering. "Well, you said you're in school taking...photography?"

"Yup, just finished my final semester in my Honours BA programme. Can't believe it's coming to an end. I feel like I've been working at it forever."

"Wow, that's exciting. What's the school like?"

"Good. You know. I'm happy I chose it. Bambi goes there, too, which is cool."

"You guys are really close, aren't you?"

Lenox nodded, wiping his lips with his napkin. "You could say that. She's amazing. My rock. I honestly don't know what I'd do without her."

"How did you guys meet?"

"Actually, our parents knew each other when they were our age. My dad was a musician and Bambi's dad was his road manager."

"No way!"

"Yup. We literally grew up together. Our parents were always on the road together."

"What? You mean like touring and shit?"

"Mm-hmm."

"Is your dad like a big deal? Would I have heard of him?"

Lenox peered at him and nodded from over his orange juice as he lifted the glass back. He shot Lyric a look that indicated he wasn't about to give that piece of information up.

"And have you thought about what happens after you graduate?" Lyric went on, despite Lenox's hesitation at giving too much away about his family.

"Oh, God, no. I've never been one to plan that far in advance!"

Lyric chewed the rest of his food, a twinkle glimmering in his eye.

"Why do you ask?" Lenox asked inquisitively, sensing there was more weight behind his question.

"Do you ever see yourself leaving the UK?"

Lenox stopped chewing for a moment as his throat tightened. He looked down at the crumbs on his plate in that nervous way he sometimes did when he wasn't sure how to answer. With no appropriate words coming to mind, despite the yearning in his gut to speak his true feelings, he decided on a simple shrug instead. Truth was that since Lenox first noticed Lyric that morning on the beach, strumming his ukulele and singing a song, he had been picturing a future with him.

Lenox was a true romantic at heart. Always had been. Growing up and watching his parents fall more in love with each other every day they were together only fuelled his desire for a happily ever after. Living in London, a city where romance and chivalry were practically non-existent, he'd begun to give up on his dreams of ever achieving what his parents had always had.

But there was something about this mysterious man whose eyes he couldn't stop staring into. Something about the way he made him feel when they were close. And certainly, something about the way Lenox's stomach flipped whenever they touched. It was certainly nothing he had ever experienced in his short dating life.

The thought of it all ending when he flew back home to reality was depressing him already. He decided to deflect this conversation that wasn't going to go anywhere good.

"What about you? Ibiza...is this where you see yourself?" His gaze flitted around the room.

Lyric paused before answering, as if truly contemplating his response. He swallowed hard and took a deep breath, the twinkle in his eye darkening a little.

"Well, nothing's written in stone, I suppose. If I'm perfectly honest—and this is something I don't think I've ever said to someone else—I think the real reason I stay is this is where my memories of my parents and Cedar are. If I were to leave, it's almost as if I'd lose a piece of them...You know?"

His response was incredibly heartfelt and made Lenox ache with sympathy.

Lenox furrowed his brow as he studied Lyric's face, which he self-consciously turned towards the ground.

"I see what you mean. But no matter where you go, you'll never lose them, Lyric, because they will always be alive in your heart..."

His words must have caught Lyric somewhere inside and he gave a tight-lipped smile.

"Cedar would have loved you," he said, changing the subject and shifting in his seat.

"Oh, really?"

"He was totally protective of me, always vetoing any potential dates before things got too serious. But I think he would have approved of you."

"Sounds like the right guy to have on your side."

"He really was."

"Do you mind if I ask something about him?" Lenox asked, unsure as to the appropriateness of the question that had burned a hole in his head ever since the other night.

"Of course!"

"Was Cedar gay, too?"

Lyric let out a laugh before turning his eyes away in that way he did to avoid showing his embarrassment.

"Uh, yes. He was."

"Really? Is that common in twins?"

"It's more common than not, from what I understand. Although, and this is not to toot my own horn or anything, he wasn't as lucky with guys as I was..."

Now, it was Lenox's turn to laugh.

"Seriously! We may have shared the same face, but he was not nearly as charismatic as I!" Lyric touched a hand to his chest in a satirical way, feigning aloofness.

"In what way?"

"Well, to be honest, I think he was a bit jealous of me...At times. He may have said he was only being protective by giving my dates the third degree, but deep down I think there was more to it than that. Like he couldn't accept that it was me getting all the attention and not him."

"Why do you think he wasn't as good on dates as you?"

Lyric paused and thought about it for a moment. "I guess he was just a bit more awkward..." He shifted yet again in that now familiar way he did when he was ready to change the subject. "So, you've not told me much about your love life."

Lenox guffawed at his remark before reaching for a serviette to wipe his mouth.

"Oh, God. What do you want to know?"

"Everything!"

Lenox breathed in deeply as it was his turn to look uncomfortable. His lips were tight and his brow furrowed as he contemplated how to respond.

"Uh-oh, did I say something..." He chewed the inside of his lip before raising his eyes and saving Lyric from his embarrassment.

"Sorry. No. Not at all. It's just...I guess to say that I've not had that much luck with relationships would be putting it mildly."

"I'm sure you're exaggerating."

"Wish I was."

"It can't be that bad...Can it?"

"Do you really want to know?"

"Only if you want to share..."

"Well, let's just say that my last boyfriend was a raging manic depressive who...How can I put this? He didn't take too well to my wanting to break up."

Lyric looked very serious all of a sudden.

"How so?"

Lenox began to well up a bit as the memories resurfaced. He debated whether or not he wanted to go into too much detail.

"After I ended it. It got pretty bad. He just couldn't accept that it was over."

Lyric could only nod, his aqua-hued eyes filled with empathy.

"He rang me obsessively. Kept showing up at my house and waiting for me outside my work. He'd follow me places and leave me threatening messages and voicemails."

"Oh, my God. Really?"

"Everywhere I went, he'd show up. It started to really scare me."

"Christ. What did you do?"

"One night, while I was walking to my car with my boss from work, he appeared out of nowhere with a baseball bat in his hand. He must have thought I was on a date or something and he started beating the shit out of him."

"Fuck, was he all right?"

"Well, luckily, my boss is quite a big guy and although he was caught off-guard he quickly regained control of the situation, if you know what I mean."

"Wow, did you report him?"

"I did more than that. I got a restraining order against him. Things were okay for a while, but about a month ago..." He paused to gather his thoughts for a moment. "About a month ago, when I got home from work late one night, he'd broken into our home."

"You're kidding?"

"Bambi wasn't home, thankfully. He must have found our spare key and was waiting for me in my room."

"In your room?"

"I almost had a heart attack. He started shouting these crazy things at me, saying that we were meant to be together and all that sort of shit. I didn't think too much of it at first, until I saw a glimpse of the knife in his hand."

Lyric, visibly stunned, could only stare in disbelief, as a silence stretched out in between them.

"He was there to kill me that night..."

With that admission, Lenox began to cry. Tears of relief. Tears that had been suppressed and tears for a time he now wished to close the door on. He wrapped his arms around himself as a way to counter the feelings he was drowning in.

"Unbelievable. Lenox, I'm so sorry."

"So am I. Unfortunately, the courts were lenient with him. Apparently, he couldn't be charged with breaking and entering seeing as he got in with a key. He got off with two years' probation."

"Fucking courts. So where is he now?"

Lenox sighed. "Well, hopefully he's still in London. Under close supervision and deeply medicated..."

"You don't sound so sure…"

A buzzing from inside the pocket of Lenox's shorts startled them both. He reached to read the display screen of his phone before quickly silencing it.

"Uh-oh, am I keeping you?"

"Sorry! No. Not at all. It's nothing. Just Bambi…"

"Oh, Jesus, she's going to think I've taken you hostage."

"Don't be silly. She's fine. We're good."

"Are you sure?"

Lenox nodded, despite the less than subtle feeling of frustration coming from her text message. She was angry. That much was obvious. And he couldn't blame her. He had been MIA these past few days. But the more Lenox contemplated things, the more he felt aloof to her concerns. This was, after all, what his friends had suggested he do.

Tucking his phone back in his shorts, he returned his gaze to Lyric. He took a deep breath as if to clear the air around them.

"Right we need a change of scenery after all this doom and gloom. What's next?" Lenox asked, officially ending his pity party.

"You sure?" Lyric asked with genuine concern.

"Absolutely."

Lyric regarded him a moment further as if assessing his expression.

"All right then. Let's shake all this off and get back to why you came to this island in the first place. You, my friend, are in for a treat."

Chapter Fifteen

THEN

After the most sumptuous breakfast at Lyric's café, and in a desperate attempt to rid themselves of all the bad mojo of their conversation, Lyric whisked Lenox off in his makeshift chariot. They stopped first in San Miguel and took a walk up to the beautiful and picturesque church in the village. Along the way, they explored the little artisan craft market where Lenox paused to appreciate the fine craftsmanship of the various Ibizan products on display. The church provided them with the most stunning overlook of the land all around and the turquoise waters that stretched well beyond the horizon.

Afterwards, it was on to Portinatx beach where Lenox gawked at the translucent waters. They two spent hours snorkelling in the bay, marvelling at the tropical sea creatures that flitted around them as they dove deep down, exploring the seabed below.

As the morning stretched into afternoon, they stopped in Cala Benirras for a late lunch at a quaint little bohemian restaurant on the beach. They gorged on a vast array of small Mediterranean plates, washed down with crisp, white wine served in a tall glass carafe.

The atmosphere of the day was nothing but entrancing as Lenox opened his eyes to a side of the island he had never dreamed about. Every which way he turned, there was a new, raw beauty that seemed buried from all the tourist guides as if it was deliberately hiding from sight and unworthy eyes. Their conversation was light and unburdened, peppered only with essential exchange, as if too much benign chatter would spoil the intensity of the beauty that surrounded them. It left Lenox with time to consider what exactly he was getting himself into. He relished the idea that Lyric was so open with him already, and with every mention of Lyric's family, he felt more drawn to this broken soul.

As they sat, Lenox stole as many lustful glances at his illustrious guide as he could without being too obvious. The energy emanating from his body was electric and Lenox was drawn to him like a moth to a flame. Lyric flashed a sideways grin in his direction that heated him from the inside out, like blowing on the dying embers of a campfire. The way Lyric made him feel was as if he was seeing a man for the first time; studying the way his body moved and contracted when he walked, the masculine set to his jawline as he spoke, and the curve of his muscles that hugged his frame in an almost poetic manner.

When they had finished eating, Lyric took Lenox by the hand and led them back to his Jeep.

"I've got one more thing to show you," he whispered into his ear and wrapped an arm around his bare shoulders.

Lenox said nothing, instead closing his eyes and breathing in the salty scent of Lyric's skin, bathing in the moment until his mouth was practically watering.

They drove east again, towards Cala San Vicente, and stopped at a small cliffside area that was deserted except for a few locals, dotted across the shaded space.

"This is one of my favourite places on the island."

Lyric took Lenox by the hand, leaving all their belongings in the car.

"Don't we need towels or anything?" Lenox asked.

Lyric did nothing but smile one of his coquettish grins in his direction, as he led him towards the beach. Despite only being late afternoon, the sun had already gone behind the surrounding cliffs of this beautiful space.

"This is called Aguas Blancas. A little secret spot only known to some of the resident hippies of the area."

"It's gorgeous," Lenox commented, his gaze skirting the cove and taking notice of the lack of swimwear adorning the revellers on the beach.

Lyric must have caught wind of Lenox's sudden anxious shift as he realised it was a nudist beach, and simply squeezed his hand and kissed his lips gently.

"Come on, you've got nothing to worry about. It's just up here..."

And with that, Lenox felt instantly at ease, as if the flow of Lyric's words washing over him had a calming effect, like auditory Valium.

After a few moments of trekking over rocky cliffs, and a short paddle through mild waters, they came upon a deserted clearing with a secluded cove. High-reaching boulders rose all around, as if guarding the secret spot from the surrounding elements. Lenox was speechless as he gazed upon the site of pure, untouched beauty that lay sprawled out in front of his eyes like a magnificent spread just for them.

"What do you think?" Lyric asked, his familiar smile appearing once again on his beautiful face.

"It's...incredible."

"Ready for a dip?"

Not waiting for a response, Lyric dropped Lenox's hand and started lifting his vest over his head as he jogged towards the shoreline. Lenox wasted no time following him, mimicking his swift strip and chucking his clothes to the ground. Lyric reached the waters first, having removed his shorts last, exposing his fantastic arse to the surrounding cliffs. Lenox paused as he untied his board shorts to marvel at the sight of Lyric wading into the water. He didn't turn around until his cock was underwater and flashed a flirtatious "come hither" look in Lenox's direction.

Lenox decided to take charge and slowed his movements down, making his reveal deliberate and seductive. Gradually he pulled down his shorts, letting them struggle as they strained over his muscular thighs before gently landing on the sand. He took a quick glance around him to inspect for any unwanted visitors before letting his hand find his own cock, sliding it over his hardening girth as he made his way into the water.

He could see Lyric's face light up and his expression shift from playful to lustful as he eyed Lenox's exploring hands.

The water was cooler than Lenox had expected, and his nipples hardened at the sudden change of temperature. He extended his tease, pausing just before the water level reached his balls, and cupping a hand into the sea to douse his chest. The water droplets traced the contours of his broad chest, heading south and glistening in the air before disappearing into the water around him.

Lyric's eyes darkened as he dipped his chin into the water, glistening like dark pools of molten chocolate. The water vibrated as his arousal seemed to ooze into the air around him. Lenox loved the feeling of being naked in the sea; a luxury he wasn't able to experience as often as he'd like. Dipping further into the water, he closed his eyes at the sensation of his cock and balls dipping unobstructed into the salty ocean.

After a moment of watching Lenox pleasure himself a few metres away from him, Lyric began inching his way towards him. His body ached for him and the thrill of being in the outdoors and all alone was making his cock twitch in excitement. Lenox opened his eyes and, as his desire erupted, threw himself into Lyric's arms.

The water splashed as their lips met and they stumbled backward, hands moving in unison and naked bodies colliding. Their skin was slick as they revelled in the new experience of exploring the other's body underwater. Lyric's hand found Lenox's cock. He jerked it feverishly underwater as he tossed his black hair back and away from his face. He grabbed Lyric's shoulders for support and wrapped his weightless legs around his waist. Lyric studied Lenox's expression, clearly gauging his reaction to the speed at which his hand moved up and down his shaft. Lenox's eyes danced behind his lids and his mouth was moulded into a wide O shape, reflecting the waves of ecstasy that flooded his frame. His legs tightened their vice grip on Lyric's waist as his hand worked Lyric's member expertly.

All around them the water splashed unforgivingly as their bodies moved with each other. Lenox's moans began to quicken and his body tensed, all his muscles contracting as if he was close to orgasm.

Lyric quickly stopped his rhythmic thrusts causing Lenox to whip his head up as if he'd been hit by a truck. Confusion slapped across his face. Lyric only mouthed "shhh" as a way of consoling him for the sudden disappointment. Smiling at him, Lyric eased his legs from around his waist until Lenox was standing up on his own again, his legs slightly weak from his near orgasm. Then, as slowly as Lenox had stripped his own clothes off, Lyric knelt down and dipped his head under the water. Lenox stilled himself as he realised Lyric's intentions. He took hold of Lyric's shoulders and guided him until he could feel his mouth open up around his cock.

The feeling caused him to cry out as Lyric took his penis into his mouth underwater. The combination of the gentle lapping waves on his bare skin and Lyric's lips wrapped around his throbbing cock was nothing short of euphoric. He struggled to find his balance as he was forced to concentrate on keeping upright. Bubbles rose to the surface of the shallow water like jets in a hot tub, tickling his legs as they swam upward.

With the sun beating down on his face and Lyric blowing him underwater, Lenox lost sight of all that was around him, very unaware of his surroundings and the possible threat of being seen or caught. His cock was close to tipping point and he knew he was about to come. He grabbed hold of Lyric's face, cupping it between his hands to signal he was about to explode. But instead of rising for air like he thought he would, Lyric kept on sucking, his tongue working away relentlessly at the head of Lenox's dick. The feeling of being sucked underwater brought him to orgasm sooner than he would have expected and he cried out his release, his sounds echoing off the surrounding boulders of the cove.

His whole body rocked and swayed as he came inside Lyric's mouth, emptying his load down the back of his throat. He relished the suction of his lips around his head as Lyric swallowed his juices, gripping his arse cheeks from behind. He sucked harder and harder as if there was something he was desperate for at the bottom of a glass, until Lenox bucked again and again, his dick sensitive and screaming out as the aftershock of the blow job swelled inside him.

Only when he was absolutely sure that he had emptied Lenox of all he had to give did Lyric rise from the water like a pornographic siren, blue eyes glistening in the sunshine and a devilish grin spread across his face. He breathed in deeply and lifted his head to kiss Lenox's lips.

Lenox returned his embrace, taking Lyric's face in his hands, and twirling his dreads around his fingers. He could taste his orgasm on his lips. Their erections grazed one another's as their bodies connected, their limbs slick and warm.

Lenox pulled back gently as he sensed Lyric's cock twinge in yearning. He was still incredibly hard and in need of release. A wry smile played with the corners of his lips as he waded across the waters to the shore. Lyric followed dutifully, his body quivering with anticipation. When they reached the sandy shore, Lenox sunk to his hands and knees, grinding his palms into the sand and anchoring himself strongly to the ground. He flaunted his arse in the air and stroked his still hard cock to invite the blood to return to his shaft. Lyric took heed and sunk to his knees behind Lenox, his stone-like erection in perfect position with Lenox's arsehole.

The air was cool against their slick bodies, but the sun began to heat them up once again as it beat down on their naked frames, licking away the quickly evaporating droplets of water. Lenox arched his back and craned his neck behind him to make eye contact with Lyric, whose expression had once again darkened with carnal pleasure.

"You sure?" Lyric whispered, his voice gruff and barely audible above the sound of the water lapping against the shore.

Lenox nodded and bit down on his bottom lip, his own body trembling. With every movement of the swelling tide, the water rose and coated Lenox's hands and knees, burying them deeper in the sand. Without hesitation, Lyric brought the head of his penis closer to Lenox and began to slide himself inside. Lenox cried out softly as he could feel himself expand against Lyric's girth. He dug his fingers into the sand, clawing at it for support against the exquisitely painful feeling of Lyric's cock entering him in one long, slow motion.

"You're so fucking tight," Lyric breathed, grabbing Lenox's hips for support as he pushed himself gently inside. "You feel so good..."

With each delectable thrust of his cock, Lenox ground his teeth more tightly together, bracing himself against the feeling, as exquisite as it was. He could feel himself expand further and further, as if his body was making more space for Lyric to be inside him. His instinct was to squeeze his buttocks together, but he fought it and forced his body to relax. He could feel Lyric's fingers digging into the skin of his hips, as he used him for leverage against the shifting sand. Lenox's knees were screaming as the sand scraped against his bare skin. For a moment, his hands gave way beneath the weight of their bodies and he lay at a forty-five-degree angle, resting on his forearms with his right cheek pressed up against the sand. The shift allowed Lyric to go deeper and he moaned in response. From the corner of his eye, Lenox could see Lyric's face; his eyes squeezed shut and his chin tipped towards the sky. His dreadlocks cascaded down his back and the muscles in his chest contracted with his every movement.

Lyric's groans got progressively more intense and his breathing quickened. Lenox could tell he was close. His hip thrusts increased in speed as he fucked Lenox harder and harder. Lenox was hard again and close to coming himself. He managed to dislodge one hand from the sand and reached around and started working away at his own cock.

"Here, hang on a sec." Lyric sensed his movement. "I want to see your face."

He withdrew his cock slowly and shifted Lenox so he was resting on his back, his black hair sprawled out around his head. He opened his legs as Lyric climbed on top of him. He took both of Lenox's ankles in his hands and used his hips to guide his dick inside him once more. He slid in easier this time, but the feeling was just as strong. Lenox writhed beneath him as he picked up speed, sucking in air between clenched teeth. His brow furrowed as surge after surge of pleasure rocked his body.

Lenox stroked his dick up and down, mimicking Lyric's movements inside him. Deeper and deeper he went with each thrust, his face twisted into a mask of complete and utter lust. His dreadlocks moved wildly around his head as he fucked Lenox hard. The air was suddenly thick and cloudy around them as if full of pheromones as the two rose together. Their bodies bucked in unison, over and over as they came together. Lenox's juices squirted all over his chest as he lost control of himself. Lyric didn't pull out, but instead came inside Lenox, his hips thrusting again and again until he had emptied himself completely.

When he finally opened his eyes, Lenox smiled up at Lyric as he bent over to kiss him on the lips. He withdrew and caressed Lenox's face softly, tracing his stubbled jawline with his fingertips before cupping his head and bringing their lips together once more.

They stayed like that, side by side, until the rising tide threatened to swallow them up. They barely spoke except for when they were collecting their clothes.

"Oh, shit!" Lenox whispered, grabbing his shorts and hiding his modesty.

"What is it?"

"Up there." He motioned towards one of the giant boulders that had been their defence against any intruders whilst they made the beach their home.

"What?"

"Behind that rock."

"What is it? I don't see anything."

But Lenox paused before responding, the tension in his body receding slightly.

"I thought I...Saw something..."

Lyric followed his gaze and shielded his eyes from the bright sky.

"There's nothing there...Promise."

And with that, he wrapped his arm around Lenox protectively and kissed his cheek. Lenox feigned a smile as he dressed, unable to prevent his gaze from skirting the area for what he thought he'd seen.

"You all right?" Lyric asked

"Yeah. Fine," Lenox lied.

"It's getting late. Shall we head out?"

Lenox nodded and gathered the rest of his stuff as they began to make their way back towards Lyric's Jeep.

Chapter Sixteen

THEN

Before long, it was dark and they ended back up back at Lyric's family apartment in the D'Alt Villa, exhausted and tired from the day they had shared. Lenox found himself dozing off as they sat on the balcony staring up at the stars. The sound of Lyric's rhythmic breathing was beginning to rock him to sleep as he lay his head on his chest and stared out at the city below.

Lenox swam in the sense of comfort and safety that floated through his body at that moment. His thoughts strayed to the last few days and a smile crept up on his face as he realised how happy he was when he was with Lyric, and how far away his twisted past seemed to be with Lyric to distract him from his wayward thoughts.

But then his thoughts drifted to his friends and how angry they must be with him for being so absent during their holiday.

How excited Bambi and he had been about getting out of London for a while. They had made so many plans together for their trip and Lenox felt he had abandoned them. He texted whenever he remembered and told them he was all right, but Bambi's one-word responses told him she was less than impressed. Guilt began to worm its way into his subconscious, but he shook it away. He knew they would be happy things were going so well with him. After all, it was the girls who'd encouraged the meet in the first instance. They could all party together anytime and anywhere. But for now, Lenox was finding himself satiated with Lyric.

He looked up into Lyric's aquamarine eyes and smiled the most genuine smile he had smiled in months.

"I don't remember the last time I was so happy," he breathed before reaching his head up for a kiss.

Lyric only smiled back and returned his kiss before returning his gaze to the sky above. Lenox felt momentarily dismissed and wished he hadn't exposed his vulnerability like he did.

A moment later, Lyric excused himself and went to the toilet. Lenox lay back feeling deflated and annoyed at himself.

His mind drifted to the day they had just spent together and the feeling he got when they were together; how warm it made him feel. Safe. Secure. So different from his relationships of the past.

His thoughts were disturbed by the sound of Lyric's phone going off on the bedside table. Curiosity getting the better of him, he reached to check the screen. With a quick swipe, the phone unlocked itself and the miniature icons came into view...

Part Two

Lyric

Chapter Seventeen

THEN

It was the pounding in his head that woke him up. As if an entire marching band was drumming along between his ears and using his brain as a punching bag. Even the thought of opening his eyes seemed like a chore. They fluttered a couple of times before stretching open into little slits, but the light that filtered through the openings was like a slice to his retinas and he recoiled his head under the duvet in self-defence.

After a couple of deep breaths Lyric tried again, slower and one eye at a time so as not to assault his senses with too much stimulation too soon.

As his vision focused and fuzzy images slowly took shape, he was struck with the panicking thought that he didn't know where he was. Furrowing his brow, he blinked again in an attempt to force his eyes into submission. After a third attempt, the panic subsided as his parents' apartment came into sight. The light that assaulted his bleary eyes was coming from the balcony doors which were wide open, a light breeze billowing in and ruffling the curtains.

He stared at the open Mediterranean-style balcony doors and felt puzzled that they had been left open after he had gone to bed. Lyric never left the doors open at night as it would be too easy for someone to climb up the fire escape and break into the apartment.

He tried brushing his concerns off and lifted himself to a sitting position, but the pain in his head only intensified when he shifted, and he almost cried out as he collapsed back down on the bed. How did he have such a searing headache? He didn't remember drinking nearly enough alcohol to warrant the pounding in his head.

When he raised his hand to rub at his temples, he noticed it.

At first, he wasn't sure what it was that coated his palms and fingers, and froze for a moment until his brain caught up with what his eyes registered. His heart followed suit, thumping away erratically inside his chest. His eyes blurred over with tears, but he was too afraid to use his hands to rub them away.

He lifted his other hand for inspection and saw that both were saturated with what appeared to be thick, red stains. The texture and coppery scent was unmistakable.

Blood.

He tore back the bed sheets in a panic. His gaze darted frantically around where he lay, worried that it was him who was bleeding, but although there were some random smudges on his bare chest, he didn't seem to be cut.

Lenox.

He swung his legs around and over the edge of the bed and stood up before ripping himself around to stare at the other side of the bed, petrified at what sight might be waiting to greet his wide eyes.

But the bed was empty.

Except for the blood.

Lyric yanked the sheets right off the bed to see the deep red stains beneath. There was an abnormally large pool of blood smeared next to where he had been lying. It petered out into smaller wisps and splodges, almost as if someone had dumped a bucket of something from high up above the bed and let it splatter around, drenching the sheets and spattering an obscenely large space around it.

"Jesus!" he cried out, recoiling from the bed until his back hit the wall behind him.

His breath hitched in his throat and his skin tingled from head to toe as he squeezed his eyes shut in an attempt to wake himself from this apparent nightmare.

But he wasn't dreaming. It was the sound of his own shallow and erratic breathing that forced him back into his body as he let go of the vain hope that he was still asleep and in the middle of some terrible dream.

He forced his eyes open to stare at the mess at his feet and counted slowly back from ten, forcing the panic back down inside him and trying to stop himself from shaking.

"No..." he murmured to the empty house around him, praying that it was some sort of sick joke. Perhaps Lenox was only hiding and waiting for the right moment to reveal himself and his practical joke and bathe in the hideous hilarity of the situation he had created.

But Lyric knew that was not the case. His gaze darted around the bedroom as he waited for the punch line that he knew would never come. The longer he stared at the blood on the bed and the splatters on the floor, the more a sort of twisted familiarity sank in.

He remained rooted to the spot until his breathing had returned to normal and the clouds in his mind had begun to clear. He steadied himself against the wall, the wheels in his head turning as a plan was formulated.

"No..." he repeated to himself. "Not again..."

Chapter Eighteen

THEN

Lyric stared out at the rising sun over the water.

He was on the beach. Some beach. Wearing only board shorts.

He looked around at his surroundings, craning his neck to see behind him, then stopped short as the muscles in his back and shoulders cried out. He rubbed the back of his neck in an attempt to soothe the shooting pains then noticed a watch on his wrist that he hadn't seen before.

It looked expensive and foreign, as if it had been imported from a posh boutique in London, not something you'd find at one of the bohemian style shops on the island. Upon closer inspection, the face read *Rolex*. He quickly unclasped it from his wrist and turned it over in his hands.

The back of the watch was inscribed and he squinted his newly awoken eyes to make it out.

To my darling Ryan,
love always,
D x

He shivered as he read the unfamiliar words then tried to remember if he knew a Ryan. Or a "D."

His head hurt. Like he had been drinking, and the moaning coming from his stomach served to tell him it had been a while since he had eaten. He looked himself over, standing up gingerly. He didn't appear physically hurt in any way and nothing seemed overtly out of the ordinary, save for his hands. He brought them up to his eyes to inspect under his nails. His hands were filthy. Dirty, as if he had been digging around in a rubbish bin, and the skin around his fingertips was cut and streaked with blood, presumably his own. But it was the deep red stains that caked the underside of his nails that worried him.

His hands trembled as he held them out in front of him and his skin prickled all over. He looked over his shoulder to see if anyone was watching him, but the beach was particularly desolate at this time of the morning. Lyric walked towards the shoreline, unsteady on his feet, and winced as the cool water washed over his bare toes. He bent down to wash his hands, rubbing them together in the salty water before splashing some over his chest, then his face. Brushing himself down, he tried to rid his skin of any signs or traces of the night before.

Or from whenever they came.

His thoughts wandered, as they habitually did whenever this happened, and he felt nauseated as he scrubbed himself over. His dreadlocks swung in front of his eyes, dipping into the water and blurring his vision further as his eyes filled with tears.

He knew he had to move quickly. He worked his way through his mental list as he had so many times before; finish wiping himself down and figure out where he was, then get home and take his meds. He tried to remember to breathe deeply to calm his nerves, for if he let himself get carried away by his thoughts he knew this wouldn't end well.

Lyric stood up and almost jogged away from the water and towards the road, keeping an eye out for any onlookers who might view his behaviour as suspicious.

Did I take my meds yesterday? Everything seemed so blurry that he couldn't be sure about anything.

He squinted his eyes to read any road signs, but it was the monolithic silhouette of Es Vedra in the distance that told him where he'd ended up. Quickly gaining his bearings, he knew he was on Cala D'Hort in the south west of the island. He forced himself to slow his speed as he found the walk that skirted the ocean and flicked his dreads away from his face in an attempt to look casual, just another local out for an early morning stroll along the beach.

The occasional passerby appeared as the sun cast its glow onto the whitewashed buildings, waking people up and announcing another new day on the island.

Lyric swallowed his fears and worries as he repeated to himself over and over that it would all be all right. If he said it enough times, he might convince himself.

Chapter Nineteen

THEN

When he found his way home, Lyric sat on his bed for almost an hour, stiff as a board and practically unmoving. Too afraid that if he stirred it might either jar memories of what had happened or alert someone to his whereabouts.

He quickly popped two tablets of his chlorpromazine, chasing it with a swig of vodka, straight out of the bottle. Not exactly the ideal way to eat his tablets, but he was desperate for something to calm his nerves.

The blinds were pulled and all his lights were off and he stared intently at his phone as if afraid it was about to spring to life and attack. But instead it stayed motionless and quiet, as though the world had forgotten about him. He willed it to remain that way. The same went for his front door; he regarded it with fear, as if someone might come looking for him and bang it down. His ears remained intensely receptive to all the sounds around him, but were greeted with nothing but quiet.

Nevertheless, his ears rung and his skin vibrated as he attempted to filter out the panic that was threatening to take hold. He tried to remember back to his counselling. *Think soothing thoughts, count down from one hundred, fill your head with white noise and try to remain calm.*

And wait for the meds to kick in.

This wasn't the first time he had woken up in a strange place, unsure of how he had gotten there or what he had done. These types of awakenings were becoming all too familiar to him.

Ever since the accident.

His parents used to think he was sleepwalking; at nighttime when he was younger he'd wander into odd places in the house—under the stairs, in the attic—and they would find him mumbling softly to himself as if in some sort of dream-state. This continued for years, until suddenly, these events seemed to stop of their own accord. Nothing more had come of them, at least nothing worthy of seeking help or a cure for them. His family simply thought he had grown out of these sleepwalking states. When he was twelve, he seemed to fall into the wrong crowd and the episodes started up again. Only this time, they were a bit more severe. He would find himself in situations that he couldn't explain and had no memory of how or what had happened.

Then his whole world collapsed.

After his parents and Cedar died when he was eighteen, something shifted inside him. He began to feel less and less like himself; irritable and angry and full of disdain. It was more than just grief. It was as if he had darkened somehow. It wasn't long after their funeral that the episodes swung into high gear. He would lash out at everyone and everything; the stealing and the violence and the blackout episodes grew worse. It all seemed like it was happening to someone else, and he was just the spectator.

Then came the time spent in the institute. It was such a confusing period of his life. He couldn't make heads or tails of what was happening to him and why they thought he did all those horrible things he was getting into trouble for.

But it wasn't up to him to try to understand *why,* as they said at the hospital, it was only important that it all stopped.

Two years of intensive therapy, confinement, group talks and exercises. When he was released he got better.

At least he thought he had.

He would take his pills at the prescribed time, check in at the prescribed time, and show up for his check-ups as they called them. For years, he felt like he was on the right track to being normal again.

Normal.

But lately the episodes seemed to be starting up again. Years down the line, things had started to shift. This time, they were more intense. Different. More disturbing.

Sometimes he'd wake up bruised or with torn clothing. Once he woke in a public park, naked except for a pair of handcuffs shackled around one wrist. Other times he'd find his pockets full of money.

But it wasn't like waking up from a dream. It was as if he was coming to. Like he had taken a holiday from his body and was only now returning to regain control of his limbs.

Lately the things he discovered in his pockets had grown more sinister. Jewellery that looked antique. Locks of hair that weren't his own. Even nail clippings.

Then there were the blood stains.

They started appearing one night a couple of years ago. They had seemed innocent enough at the time. Cuts and blood on his fingertips or knees that he thought were due to having fallen during one of his episodes; the occasional graze on his forehead or nose. But then one night he woke up in an underground parking garage in the backseat of a car that he didn't recognise. When he began his inspection of himself, it didn't take long before he saw his top and arms were streaked with blood. Too much blood to be accidentally spilled.

And it wasn't his own.

Then there was the matter of the missing persons reports. Four in the last eight years. Young men, gay men like himself, all under the age of thirty and all missing on the island. All missing in areas where he would inexplicably find himself during one of his episodes.

Lyric knew he should have gone to the police years ago. But he was too afraid they'd have him locked up again. He was terrified of what truth he might discover about himself. He detested his time in the Institute and there was no way in hell he'd ever go back. Not over his dead body.

There was no denying the cowardly fashion in which Lyric lived his life. He knew he should have sought help after the first incident. Turned himself in or at least gone to the police for help. But he didn't. And he knew he never would. He always kept an eye on the local news, each day waking up and praying that no missing persons would have been reported and that he could live another day of his life without worrying he'd be caught for something he had no memory of doing.

Lying to himself had become a part of his daily routine.

He shook his head and stood abruptly.

This was not the time to head down memory lane, not while in this state. This was the time to remain in control. Calm. Present.

He showered twice. Each time letting the water run so hot that it practically scalded his skin, leaving it red and raw. He scrubbed himself from head to toe, desperate to feel clean and normal; the fear of the unknown plaguing him and making his stomach turn. He vomited twice before forcing a piece of toast down his throat in an effort to stop the shakes that were taking over his frame.

Once dressed and somewhat presentable, he stood in his lounge, staring around, unsure of what to do with himself. He spied his ukulele in the corner of the room, propped up against a table that held a vintage record player; one of the many things in the apartment left over from his parents' day.

His parents had instilled in him a love of music and taught him how to play the piano, ukulele, and guitar among other things. Since he had been young, music was his escape. Ibiza was the perfect place to harbour a love and adoration for all things musical and since his episodes had recommenced in his early twenties, Lyric had found solace and comfort in his instruments.

The sight of his ukulele was enough to still his thoughts, even for a moment, and allow him to partially convince himself that everything was going to be all right.

He strode over to the table and picked up his uke, before heading straight for the door, knowing there was only one place for him to go.

Chapter Twenty

THEN

The sun was just starting to show itself in the rosy sky, therefore the beach wasn't busy when Lyric made his way down. He walked towards the shore as if in a trance, eyes fixed on the ground and taking no notice of those around him. His feet were bare and he wore only a pair of shorts despite the slight chill to the air, but his skin was neither warm nor cold, as if he had lost all feeling in his body.

When he reached the sand, he fell into a lounge chair listlessly, exhausted yet buzzing at the same time. His mind had settled and begun to clear itself, letting go of the anxiety and trying to remain still and untethered, yet his chest felt heavy and dull and plagued with a sense of worry and doubt that he couldn't shake.

Lyric let his head fall back and rest on the lounger as he exhaled deeply, closed his eyes, and began to play. It only took a moment for his fingers to find their way on the strings of the instrument, plucking them gently and coaxing soothing vibrations from its wooden curves. His lips moved to the words of a sweet melody that he shared with the ocean before him. His skin warmed as the rising sun greeted him and told him it would be all right.

Music took him away. Away from his thoughts and out of his head. When he was alone with his music, it was as if nothing could touch him. All his many worries and fears simply melted away and his mind became calm and still.

After a few moments of being lost in his little world, Lyric had the feeling he was being watched. Opening his eyes, he was greeted by the sight of someone standing before him. It jarred him at first glance, worry immediately flooding his body as to who this stranger might be. But as he relaxed and took in the situation, he quickly realised he needn't have been concerned. For on the face of the man standing before him wasn't an accusatory or angry expression, but a look of lust.

Lyric continued to play his instrument, only this time with his eyes open. He gazed upon the lone member of his audience, soaking up the sight and appreciating the distraction. He loved to play for an audience, however small or diverse. Secretly he loved being the centre of attention. He yearned for it—eyes on him, drinking him in. He relished the focus.

The man watching him was young. Perhaps a few years younger than Lyric. He had long, jet-black hair pulled back in a low bun at the nape of his neck. He was dressed casually, but his appearance and the way he seemed to hold himself betrayed him as a tourist. Lyric let a small grin inch its way up his face as a way of keeping his attention. He eyed his slim, yet full physique, feeling its effect resonate between his legs. There was a sudden tension between them and Lyric waited for the stranger to return his smile. But instead he seemed to become very self-aware and he turned and continued walking down the beach.

Disappointment flooded his whole body. As fast as it had started, the moment faded away and Lyric was left alone on the beach chair, the feeling of emptiness and fear creeping back up again inside him. He waited and watched as the guy faded away into a shapeless form before he got swallowed up by the surroundings further along the beach.

Lyric's smile faded away as well, and he once again closed his eyes as he remembered why he was here.

He remained there on the beach chair for the better part of an hour, until the building sounds of the people around him forced his eyes back open. He stretched his limbs and looked towards the shoreline.

Something dark and metallic caught his eye. It was just on the edge of the water, about to be swallowed up by the rising tide. Lyric strode over to it and picked it up.

It was a mobile phone. Black casing, simple and yet stylish. He surveyed his immediate surroundings for any sign of someone looking for a lost phone, but there wasn't anyone remotely close to the water's edge. When he pressed the home key, the screen lit up to reveal a photo of a man and four women, posing for a picture, all pouty lips and glazed eyes. It was the man's face that caught his attention. He was beautiful, with almond-shaped eyes the colour of black coffee and big black brows. His hair was dark and swept back off his face. It appeared to be tied back at the nape of his neck.

Lyric stared at his face a moment longer before he recognised him as the stranger who'd been watching him play. He looked around himself in hope, his stomach coming to life and a boyish excitement reaching his every nerve ending. He checked for a locked screen, but to his surprise with a swipe of his finger the phone unlocked itself, the familiar icons presenting themselves for his viewing pleasure.

A sly smile played with the corners of his lips as he turned to go, taking the phone with him.

Chapter Twenty-One

THEN

When he got back to his apartment, Lyric took a sleeping tablet and lay down. Curled up in his bed, he slept without dreaming, plagued by the same familiar sense of anxiety and nervousness he always experienced after an episode. The air inside his apartment was warm, and a simple white sheet covered his naked frame.

When he finally stirred from his sleeping pill haze, the sky outside his bedroom window was black and the afternoon heat long gone. He shivered beneath the thin sheet and quickly moved to cover himself with the robe hanging on the door of the en suite bathroom. He hugged his arms around him as he walked drowsily towards his open window, the floor-length white sheer curtains billowing in the evening breeze.

He ran a hand through his dreads and gathered them behind his neck, as he surveyed the throngs of people on the streets below. He caught a few of their glances as his thoughts strayed to the dark-haired stranger from this morning.

And his phone that Lyric had picked up from the beach.

He turned to where he had set it on the bedside table and checked the notification screen and saw eight missed calls. All intermittently placed over the past couple of hours from someone the man had saved in his contacts as simply "'B'."

Having scrolled through his texts he came to find out that the guy was called Lenox. And whoever he was, he was bound to be searching the beach for his phone.

The beach...

Lyric checked the large clock on the wall across the open-plan lounge.

Twelve-thirty.

He threw on a pair of swimming trunks and a plain white vest, grabbed his keys and both his phone and the one he had found on the beach, and set off.

WHEN LYRIC ARRIVED at his destination, he wondered if this was a stupid move. The beach was peppered with shadowy figures, all enjoying the late-night warmth and chilled-out vibe by the sea. He sat near the water's edge and looked back towards the groups of people, straining his eyes to spot *him*. As the minutes passed, Lyric realised the chances of him being down here at this exact time were slim to none. But something in his gut told him to wait.

After an hour of listening out in vain for a foreign accent, Lyric decided to take a quick dip and call it a night. He peeled off his vest and walked into the water. There was a slight chill to the sea that felt good against his skin as he dunked himself under, letting the small waves wash over his head.

For a moment, all was quiet. Not only was the noise from the beach dimmed, but also the sounds from inside his head. Under the water, all was still and time seemed to follow suit. Lyric kicked his legs and swam out a bit to escape even further from the demons that awaited him back at shore. He allowed himself to forget all the plaguing worries about his condition. When he surfaced, he looked back at the bright lights of Ibiza's shoreline, and took a moment to appreciate its beauty even when bathed in shadow.

He stayed afloat for a while until the fire in his legs from treading water became too strong to ignore and forced him back to shore.

When his feet could feel the sand, he walked out of the water, letting the droplets drip down off his broad chest as he inched his way out. As he shook the excess water from his dreads his gaze fell upon a group of people just off to his left. He squinted in the darkness. It looked like a guy and a couple of girls. He stood still for a moment, letting the air dry his body and realised that they, whoever they were, were looking towards him and giggling in a very schoolgirlish sort of way.

One of them yelled something in his direction in what sounded like a British accent. Something about having "nice abs," followed by lots of shushing and more giggling.

It was him. Lenox. From earlier. It had to be. Although his face was awash in shadow, Lyric could see the shine coming from his black hair that was drawn messily back into a bun. He was dressed in a smart button-down shirt with the sleeves rolled up to his elbows.

And he was looking this way.

Lyric decided to take a chance. He pulled the vest over his head and grabbed the two phones he had brought with him, then slowly made his way over to where the group sat.

There were some hushed mutterings as they silenced each other. Lyric took a deep breath and flashed his most award-winning smile.

"*Esperaba verte de nuevo*," he said in Spanish, knowing full well Lenox probably didn't speak the language.

"I'm sorry, what's that?" Lenox responded, a look of total confusion on his face.

"Oh, apologies," Lyric said, placing a hand to his chest, "I'm not sure why I assumed you were Spanish. Forgive me." He lied through his enormous grin.

The girls, as well as Lenox, seemed at a loss for words as they sat there, clearly stunned by Lyric's attempt to be chivalrous. "I was just saying I was hoping to see you again."

"Oh," Lenox muttered.

Lyric held out an iPhone. "I think this belongs to you…"

Chapter Twenty-Two

NOW

"Why don't you tell us about your time at L'Institut Pere Mata?" the male officer asked, his tone somewhat mocking.

But he only returned the question with silence.

"Mustn't have been a very fun time for you," the female officer added, her gaze down on the file in front of her. "Looks like you spent most of your time there in solitary confinement."

He flinched again. The memories of his time there flooded back with an unwelcome veracity. He closed his eyes and tried counting down from one hundred, as he had so many times before, but could already feel himself beginning to fade away in that all-too-familiar way. The ringing in his ears overwhelmed him, as did the sensation of weightlessness. He gripped the chair beneath him as if it would help anchor him to his body, the officers' monotone drones quieting and fading away into hushed static.

"Lyric..."

The effect of that word was like a crack of a whip inside his head. It was the first time she had used his name since they had sat down. The sound of it jarred him further and suddenly he was back in the room. He looked down at his hands, counting his fingers and pinching the skin on his forearm; a trick he had learned in the hospital to bring him back to the present moment and out of whatever state he was in. The rising panic slowly subsided as did the ringing in his ears.

He raised his head to look them both in the eye, his previous arrogant manner gone, replaced by a look of fear and uncertainty. Tears pooled behind his eyes, prickling their way out to the surface and spilling down over his lids.

"Lyric...do you remember much about your time at the L'Institut Pere Mata in Reus, Catalonia?"

The female officer's manner had shifted, as well, as if she too could detect the change in atmosphere. She assessed him with wide eyes, leaning forward in her chair and resting her hands on the table between them. Her expression softened as she took Lyric in, like a mother would regard another person's child who was in some sort of pain.

Lyric studied her face in return as if seeing her for the first time. He opened his lips to speak, but couldn't find his voice. He swallowed air and tried again, but still his throat felt dry and closed.

She waited a moment further before sitting back and pulling out a report from the file she was clutching. She placed it in front of Lyric so he could read.

His bleary eyes drifted down to the document, noticing the hospital stamp first at the top of the page. He scanned it without really reading it, words jumping off the page at him but bouncing back as if not having much of an effect.

"Lyric, when you first arrived at the Institute, following the death of your family, you were diagnosed with Dissociative Identity Disorder...Do you remember that?"

The answer to her rhetorical question was obvious.

How could he forget?

Every time he closed his eyes, he could hear the voices of his doctors; their questions; the prick of the needles in his arms; the therapy sessions; the tests. Try as he might, there was no way he would ever be able to forget a single minute of his time at the hospital, let alone the condition that would plague him for the rest of his days.

Dissociative Identity Disorder.

How he had gotten so good at dealing with doctors. How he had managed to win over the people looking after him. Day by day. Moment by moment, he was always busy. Knowing that if he were ever to see the other side of these hospital walls there was work to be done. Tales to be spun. Skills to be crafted if he were to convince them all that the voices had faded away...

"Lyric, I'm afraid it's time we got down to the reason we're all here." The male voice startled him at first.

"Lyric," the female officer said, picking up where her companion left off, "can you tell us about Cedar..."

Chapter Twenty-Three

THEN

That night, after their kiss, and after Lenox left him on the beach, Lyric stood rooted to the spot, watching his figure grow increasingly smaller until he disappeared into the shadows. His gut was screaming out in agony at his head for letting Lenox go, but it was fear that held him back.

Fear had become a part of his daily routine these days and he figured that Lenox was better off keeping his distance. The thought of getting close to someone and putting them at risk was too much for him to fathom.

And yet, later that night, it was all he could think about. No matter how brief their meeting had been, there was no denying the connection he felt towards him already. Their conversation had flowed so easily and it was the most at ease he had felt in a while.

Just like all those times before.

Perhaps it was simply his mind's way of coping with the palpable loneliness he struggled with, but he was desperate to feel something other than fear. His heart ached for the touch of another. Something real and gratifying that he could hold onto. But he knew that if he let someone in then he put them at risk.

It was another sleepless night for Lyric, filled with endless tossing and turning. His head rocked back and forth with thoughts and questions and visions of Lenox.

The clock next to his bed read quarter to six the last time he checked, and the next time he opened his eyes, it was just past ten. Giving in, he pulled himself out of bed, quickly showered and left the house.

He wasn't sure exactly at what point he had decided on seeing Lenox again during the night, but as his feet hit the pavement, he didn't give it another thought.

WHEN HE ARRIVED at the beach, guitar in hand and wearing nothing but his usual board shorts and a tie-dye vest, he scanned the many different groups of people who were already on the beach at this early hour. It only took a moment for him to spot a group of four girls, each in tiny bikinis and with assorted coloured hair; the same group he had met on the beach last night with Lenox. He wasted no time in going over to them.

As he approached, his bare feet padding their way through the deep, golden sand, their animated conversation came to a close and they stared at him.

"*Buenos días*," he offered to them with a wide, toothy grin.

A short silence filled the space between them before one of the blondes cleared her throat and returned his greeting.

"*Buenos días,*" she replied, her voice a mixture of what he imagined to be posh English and a half-hearted attempt at a Spanish accent.

"Please forgive me, *señoritas*, if I am bothering you," Lyric added, his hands together in a prayer position in front of his heart.

"Not at all," the ginger one said. "You looking for Lenox? 'Cause the lazy ass is still in bed..."

Lyric gave a gentle laugh, meeting her eyes with his own friendly stare before continuing.

"I'm afraid you've pinned me already. I was, in fact, looking for Lenox. Do you expect him to be joining you today?"

The ladies all looked at Lyric in awe, lapping up his chivalrousness and kind nature; exactly the way he had intended.

"Here's hoping," the ginger one said.

"I'm Bambi," the blonde offered, licking her lips.

"Lyric," he replied. "A pleasure to make all of your acquaintances."

"Would you care to join us, Lyric?" another blonde asked, her voice much lighter than the first.

"I wouldn't want to intrude."

"You wouldn't be," Bambi interjected.

"No. But thank you very much for the offer. Really."

"It's no bother, honestly. I'll text Lenox and I'm sure he'll come right down."

"No, no, please. I'd actually like to surprise him. I wouldn't want him to feel forced to meet me. After last night, I mean..."

The girls all exchanged confused glances before turning back to Lyric.

"I'll just wait over there. Again, it was lovely to meet you. All of you." Lyric took his guitar and moved away silently, flashing them all another quick smile before tossing his dreads over his shoulders and making his way over to a lounger.

A half hour or so passed before Lenox joined the girls on the beach. Lyric noticed his jet-black hair first, tied once again in a knot at the back of his head. He wore a casual pair of navy-blue swimming trunks and a black vest that framed his broad shoulders to perfection. He carried only a towel with him, draped around his neck, and spoke in an animated manner to his friends.

Lyric tried to play it cool, strumming his guitar casually as he watched the scene unfold from the corner of his eye. After a moment or two, he felt sets of eyes on him. Pretending not to notice, he continued playing, adding Spanish lyrics to a made-up song as he turned his own gaze to the sea.

After a few minutes, he spied a figure coming towards him in his peripheral vision. He remained draped across the sun lounger as if he hadn't a care in the world.

When Lenox was finally a few feet in front of him, he turned to face him; a sly, sideways smile tugging at one corner of his lips.

"*Buenos días,*" he said in his raspy tone.

"Good morning," Lenox responded in English.

"Your friends said you'd be along soon enough."

"Have you really been waiting here for *me*?"

Lyric nodded, squinting up at him through the harsh light of the sun. He patted the seat next to him, inviting Lenox to sit.

"How are you?" Lenox asked, accepting the invitation and taking a seat next to him.

"I'm good, thanks, how are you feeling?"

"Yeah, feeling all right. I guess." He leaned forward, resting his forearms on his thighs, and steepled his hands. "Look, I'm sorry for last night..."

"Sorry for what?"

"Sorry for shooting off in a huff...I guess I had a bit too much to drink."

"No worries, I'm glad I got to see you again."

"You are?"

"Sure! Why wouldn't I be?"

"Well, I thought...I guess I just assumed when you didn't want to..."

"What, get a bite to eat?"

"Well, yeah…"

Lyric felt relaxed, and very sure of himself. He could sense Lenox's unease and he was finding it irresistibly sexy. He leaned in, closing the distance between them a fraction. With his hand, he pulled Lenox's face towards his own until they were once again eye to eye.

"I just didn't want to do something I'd regret and that you wouldn't remember," he whispered, his lips barely moving as they caressed each word.

"Something you'd regret?" Lenox repeated his words back to him.

"Well, less that I'd regret, and more that you wouldn't remember enough to appreciate…"

And with that, Lyric pulled his face in for a kiss, planting his lusciously full lips on Lenox's mouth.

Lyric sensed his nerves, Lenox holding back as if he was afraid to take it too far, or let himself go somehow. But he only pulled Lenox in closer as a way of trying to rid him of his doubt. Finally, Lenox met his intensity and returned it with the same fire.

Their lips parted and Lyric pushed his tongue into Lenox's mouth. It was warm and wet and searching. Lenox found Lyric's face with his hands and gently traced the line of his jaw from his chin to the back of his head until they reached his mane of thick dreadlocks.

The feeling of Lenox's hands on his face switched Lyric on like a lightbulb and he returned the gesture, letting his hands find Lenox's face, his fingertips dancing across his stubbled cheeks and tangling themselves in his long black hair. Lyric began to stiffen in his shorts, the material tugging and constricting as his erection grew with each stroke of his tongue inside Lenox's mouth.

He pulled Lenox's face in closer still, their noses touching and heads tilting to opposite sides to make room for their kiss. Lenox shifted his body, causing the chair to creak beneath their weight. He seemed to get spooked and pulled away from their embrace.

Licking his lips, he looked quickly away, scanning the beach for gawkers.

"I'm sorry…I'm not usually so…"

"Don't be," Lyric interrupted, casting a glance around him. "Take a look. I don't think anyone even blinked an eye. This is Ibiza, after all!" He sat back in a casual pose, bending one knee and tucking it up underneath him on the chair.

Lenox turned to face him, smiling enormously.

"Listen, I don't want to keep you from your friends, but I was wondering...do you have any plans for dinner tonight?" Lyric asked.

"Tonight?"

"Because I'd love to take *you* out for that bite."

"That would be...Great."

"Excellent. Shall I pick you up around nine?"

"Yes, sounds perfect."

Lenox plugged the address of the villa where he was staying and his number into Lyric's phone before wishing him a good day as Lyric stood to leave.

Lyric walked away elated, filled with happiness and wishing this feeling would stay with him. He closed his eyes as he wandered down the promenade, the stone warm beneath his bare feet. He tried to push his fears and nerves deep down into his core, projecting them and all other negativity out and back down into the earth.

Perhaps this time will be different. Perhaps this time, I'll be able to keep control.

Perhaps this time, no one will get hurt.

Chapter Twenty-Four

THEN

After their dinner at Teatro Pereyra, Lyric was on top of the world. Their conversation had been so easy, so pleasant. He was finally starting to feel like himself again.

He decided to bring Lenox back to the apartment in the D'Alt Villa. Once inside, the sexual vibe between them seemed to crank itself up a notch. Lyric stared at Lenox as he explored the apartment, taking in the view from the floor-to-ceiling Mediterranean-style windows. He admired his beautiful, muscular frame; the way his chest rose with each breath he took, the muscles in his legs flexed as he casually shifted the weight from one to the other.

As Lyric stood on the spot, the onset was quick this time. So quick he barely had time to react, let alone to put up a fight. Within seconds he was floating up above his body, looking down at himself, the sounds in the apartment replaced by a piercing ringing in his ears. He could still feel his limbs but it was as if he was no longer in control of them. His mouth tasted differently too and there was a new smell to his skin that was so subtle only he could detect it. He heard his voice excuse himself as his body made its way into the bedroom.

He watched from above as his hand dipped into his shorts and pulled out his mobile and dialled a number.

Who am I calling? And why?

Still floating up above, he believed if he tried hard enough he could strain to see who he was calling.

It was Lenox's number appearing on the display screen.

The surreal nature of what was happening made his head throb. It was as if he was a passenger in his own body, and someone else was in the driver's seat. He was helpless to stop it, and could only sit back and watch the story unfold. He felt so far away from his body and the feeling only intensified as the seconds ticked by. Before long the images he was watching began to blur and fade around the edges as if he was floating further and further away from the scene. The clouds in his head went from white to grey to black.

He recognised the smell his skin had taken on. It was both familiar and strange, like something from his past but also linked somehow to his present.

Vanilla.

It was Cedar's smell. The scent of his aftershave. The scent of his skin. So poignant and so present. Right here in his nostrils. Filling the room with its sweet musk. Back from the grave.

Then he was gone.

Chapter Twenty-Five

NOW

"Cedar and I were always so different," Lyric began, focusing his attention at his hands in his lap, unable to look at the officers anymore. "You'd think identical twins would be more on the same page than we were, but nothing about us was similar. Not our tastes, not the way we dressed, not even the way we wore our hair. I remember the day I got my dreads done, Cedar was so disgusted with me he couldn't even look at me for a week. But despite how different we were, we were completely and totally inseparable."

"Did you have the same group of friends?" the female officer asked.

"Cedar didn't really have many friends. I was always the outgoing one, whereas he preferred his own company. I would always ask him to join me if I was going somewhere. Sometimes he would, but when he did, he would always seem awkward and uncomfortable. Like he would rather be anywhere but there. He much preferred it when we did things together...Alone."

"Would you say that your brother was possessive of you?"

Lyric paused and thought about the question before answering.

"Possessive doesn't even begin to describe it."

"How so?"

"As we became teenagers, I sort of fell into the wrong crowd. I started hanging with the popular kids our age on the island. Getting into trouble, drinking, drugs, that sort of thing. Cedar hated it. He hated that I started spending so much time away from him."

"So, he was hurt?"

"He was destroyed. We started growing apart. He would become angry with me for no reason; we'd fight. Throw things."

"Was he ever physically violent towards you?"

"I'm not sure who started it, but yeah. We were both quite violent with each other at times."

"What changed?"

"I started getting into trouble a lot. Like serious shit. I started getting sent away…"

"To detention centres?"

Lyric just nodded.

"And how did Cedar feel about you going away?"

Lyric sighed before answering, "Although he never actually came out and said it, I think he was almost happy I was getting sent away…"

"He wasn't upset at losing you again?"

"Part of him was…But another part of him was happy seeing me suffer."

The officers exchanged a look between themselves.

"He was happy I was hurting. Pleased that I was finally learning my lesson. Once when he came to visit me in juvie, he had the smuggest look on his face, like I was getting what I deserved."

"How did that make you feel?"

"I hated feeling like the black sheep of the family."

"Did it change the way you acted when you got out?"

"When I got out of juvie, you'd think it would have set me on the straight and narrow. I wanted to be good. I really did. I tried to be good…"

"But?"

"But it was as if I wasn't totally in control. You know? Like there was something stopping me from changing. Like there was something in me that wanted to see me suffer."

Lyric picked at the skin around his thumb until it started to bleed. He sucked it before sitting back in his chair and running a hand through his dreadlocks.

A silence stretched out between them as the officers considered the next direction they wished to take.

"Lyric, tell us about the accident."

Chapter Twenty-Six

THEN

When Lyric awoke the next morning, he felt disorientated and fuzzy, as though he was waking up in someone else's bed after a one-night stand. Shifting where he lay, it took a moment for his eyes to refocus and for the familiar surroundings to come to light.

Feeling something in the bed next to him, he turned to see Lenox lying there, sound asleep and snoring softly. He froze for a moment as his head caught up with what his eyes were seeing.

What is Lenox doing in my bed?

He began to shake as he was coming up blank.

Yanking himself out of bed, he could do nothing but stare at Lenox's body, framed beautifully beneath the thin white sheet.

He stared as he desperately tried to remember. Thinking back. Trying to piece together what he remembered about the night before.

What happened and how did we end up in bed together? Did we have sex? Why can't I remember?

He could recall snippets. They were by the window. It was late. After dinner. He had brought Lenox back to the apartment and they were admiring the view...

But then what?

The feeling.

He remembered that feeling of weightlessness. He remembered leaving the room and excusing himself for a minute. Dialling a number. Lenox's number.

Then the smell of vanilla.

But that was it. That was the last thing he could remember.

He stared down at Lenox asleep in his bed. Naked. He had no memory of when or how they had gotten there, and the more he allowed his mind to try to recollect the details, the more forceful the panic became. It started off slow and unmoving, like a rock sitting in the pit of his stomach. He could sense an attack on its way.

Shaking his head, he grabbed a pair of briefs from the floor. He wrapped his dreads into a pile on his head before securing them with an elastic band from around his wrist, and set off for the kitchen.

He poured himself a glass of freezing cold water from a bottle in the fridge and drank it down in one, the cool liquid awakening his core and settling his impending panic attack. He counted down from one hundred in his head and waited for the panic to subside and the shakes to stop. Opening his eyes and gripping the countertop for support, he fished around in his head for answers.

His mind was blank. Completely void as to what had happened last night. His chest was still gripped with anxiety and he began to quiver with fear and uncertainty.

He needed to be busy. His hands could not be idle or the paranoia that was nestled in his belly would take hold and he'd fall apart.

Which was something he couldn't let himself do in front of Lenox.

Not today. Not yet. Not after an episode.

How would he explain it? Lenox would think he was deranged and be out of his life faster than he had come into it. But as he moved around his open-plan kitchen, he told himself that this was not going to be the case. Not again. Not like the last time.

Breakfast. He would make them breakfast. They would eat and everything would be okay. Lenox was fine. Nothing bad had happened. He poured himself another glass of water from the fridge and drank it faster than before. He was starting to feel better. Calmer.

It wasn't long before he heard shuffling coming from the bedroom. Lenox was up. He put a smile on his face and prepared a whole conversation in his head as he did sometimes when he was nervous.

Lenox appeared around the corner a moment later, looking ruffled and sleepy.

"¡*Buenos días!*" he called out, flashing Lenox a forced, toothy grin.

"Good morning."

"I hope you're hungry. French toast?"

Chapter Twenty-Seven

NOW

"What do you want to know? Everything you need is in the police report I had to give."

"We're not interested in the police report, Lyric. We want to know what really happened."

"Well, I wasn't there..."

A beat passed between them, almost as if the officers didn't believe him.

"I wasn't. I don't know what happened. They had an accident."

"Why weren't you with them that night?"

Now, it was Lyric's turn to pause. A long heavy pause that spoke volumes without uttering a word. Lyric shifted in his chair, feeling warm and suddenly uncomfortable in his own skin.

"Lyric, what happened the night of the accident?" she repeated.

"We had gotten in a fight."

"Can you be more specific?"

"I had just gotten home. It was dark. I was high as a kite. I had gotten into an accident in the car and smashed the whole front. All the lights were out and broken. Cedar was so angry with me. Disappointed. He kept calling me worthless, and a waste of space."

"Go on."

"We fought. Like we had been so much lately. I had been really trying to get my act together. I felt like my last stint in juvie had put me straight. But then that night I was out with some mates and got wrecked and crashed the car while trying to pull out of a parking spot. So stupid."

He felt the sting of tears behind his eyes once more.

"Cedar had been waiting for me to get home so he could pick up our parents from a party they were at. I was late. Obviously. He stormed out of the house and got in the car to go pick them up. I didn't think anything of it, until it dawned on me that he'd be driving in the dark with no lights..."

"You let him drive the smashed car..."

"He shouldn't have. He said it wasn't that far and he didn't have money for a taxi. I should have stopped him."

"What happened, Lyric?"

"He was gone for over an hour. He should have been back by then, but he wasn't. I was still so fucked up, I didn't realise what time it was. I had passed out on the sofa watching TV and..."

"And?"

"And then I got the call. The police. They had found the car."

The female officer looked down and read from the official report. "The driver, Cedar Reed, aged eighteen, and passengers Linda and Stephen Reed, both fifty-five, were killed on impact as their vehicle collided with a passing vehicle on the highway between Cala Llonga and Cala San Vicente at approximately 9:15 P.M. The family were travelling in a Toyota Yaris that had sustained substantial damage to the front bonnet in a previous accident and was without the use of functioning headlights. The driver of the other vehicle was unharmed..."

Lyric was quiet, except for the sound of his tears that came more freely now, rolling down his face and pooling in his cupped hands in his lap. The words from the report pelted him like hailstones as the officer read them out robotically and without any human emotion.

He remembered being called out to the accident. Identifying the bodies of his brother and parents. He remembered the feeling of emptiness and loss that had encased his every nerve. He remembered being on the brink when a police officer drove him to the scene.

He closed his eyes now and he could still see the wrecked car, the spilled blood; hear the wail of the sirens. He could see the bodies laid out on slabs in the morgue like show pieces at a deranged art gallery. He remembered the feeling of emptiness. Such hollow emptiness, as if all emotion and feeling had been drained out of him, dying with his family.

His family.

As Lyric sat there now before the officers, he wiped a hand across his face and nose, ridding it of the tears that exposed him for the vulnerable victim he'd started to feel like.

Cedar. His mother. His father. The institute. It was all too much. He wanted to forget, not to remember. He didn't want to go there again. Not after he'd worked so hard to push the memories down. It was the only way to survive. The only way to remain *him*.

He closed his eyes again, squeezing them tight. He started counting down from one hundred and clasped his hands tight together in his lap, praying that the panic would subside.

He straightened in his chair, wrung his hands and looked up.

But when his eyes met with those of the officers seated across from him, something shifted. The two figures began to blur before him, their edges becoming fuzzy, and their features became lost in a cloudy haze. Then he smelled it.

Vanilla.

A sweet waft that filtered through his nostrils and made his body feel weightless, like some sort of toxic helium. He tried fighting it. Tried to refocus his eyes and return to his counting. But it was futile. He was already drifting from where he sat, looking down on himself and the officers, an observer on the situation, a third party in the room. The blackness was almost here.

His features twisted somehow, his eyes darkening and changing shape slightly. His mouth moved and inched into a sideways grin that was more menacing than pleasant. He sat forward for the first time since the interview started and he began to drum his fingers impatiently on the Formica table, the sound disturbing the silence and visibly startling the officers, who sat back as if animals protecting themselves from a predator.

The energy in the room shifted, as did the dynamic, as the interviewee seemed to supersede the interviewers.

No one moved for a moment. There was a battle of the wills as the officers stared at this new presence before them in surprise and awe, unsure as to what had just happened.

The female officer was the first to speak.

"Lyric?" she attempted through tight lips.

But he didn't move. He didn't blink. He just continued to stare, more between the two of them than directly at them. The officers exchanged nervous glances as they silently reassessed the situation at hand.

She opened her mouth to try again.

"With whom am I speaking?"

Chapter Twenty-Eight

THEN

Lyric was escorted home by an officer after identifying the bodies at the Hospital Can Misses in Ibiza town, and dropped off at the apartment he shared with his family.

Had shared...

The officer had asked if he would be all right on his own, to which Lyric had only grunted in response. The grief counsellor at the hospital had requested Lyric stay overnight at the hospital for observation, but he had refused.

He wanted out of there. They had asked if he had anyone whom they could call to notify or who could come and pick him up. But he had no one. No one was left. This had been it. His whole family.

Lyric's movements were almost robotic as he passed through the many minders at the hospital, signing papers and documents. Flashing his ID whenever needed and answering questions he could not now remember. There was so much paperwork and red tape to clear that he just switched off as his way of dealing with everything. His hands felt numb as did his legs. He was simply going through the motions in a dream-like state of unawareness, counting down the seconds until he could be alone again to process all that had happened. When he closed his eyes the noises around him turned to static and left him with an odd sense of comfort despite the hellish scenario. He longed to stay there longer and just let himself drift away. But it wasn't long before someone interrupted his trance and plagued him with something else he had to attend to.

When it was all over, at least for that moment, he was permitted to leave, as long as he checked back in with the hospital first thing in the morning for an evaluation.

As the officer drove him back to his house, the road seemed different somehow. Almost alien. The curves were unfamiliar and the sounds otherworldly. He allowed himself to rest his head on the window and look up at the inky-dark sky. Even the stars seemed to dull, despite the clearness of the night, and the thrumming of the engine mirrored the throbbing in his head.

When they arrived at his home, he and the officer parted ways and exchanged emotionless pleasantries. It was as he closed the front door, and the darkness surrounded him, that he lost control.

He smelled the vanilla first. Strong and sweet like someone had placed a vial of smelling salts directly beneath his nose. It was so immediate that he flinched as the scent invaded his nostrils, making his head swim.

"Cedar?" he cried out. For vanilla was his twin's signature scent. Always had been. Cedar had adored it ever since they were little, demanding that all the candles in the apartment be vanilla scented. He loved vanilla ice cream, vanilla soda. Even vanilla perfume—which Lyric had always teased him about as it was such a female-associated scent.

But as his bleary eyes searched the darkness, he didn't expect to find Cedar there, despite the odd smell in the air. The throbbing in his head was getting worse and it persisted until it developed into a ringing in his ears that got so loud and unbearable he had to shut his eyes and grit his teeth.

Dropping to his knees, both out of exhaustion and from the sound in his head, he opened his eyes in an attempt to centre himself and was surprised to find his vision so out of focus. He reached for a light switch and flicked it on in hopes of clarifying the misshapen surroundings of his home.

But the lights only made it worse. Everything blurred until a sort of halo surrounded the furniture in his lounge. He rubbed at his eyes to clear them, but it was a fruitless attempt. The panic came next. A fear that wormed its way through him, leaving his limbs shaking and cold.

A moment later, he was floating. Weightless. Like a feather drifting in the breeze. He watched as his stiff body grew smaller beneath him as he seemingly rose above himself until he was able to look down upon his blurred frame. It was as if he had been pushed out of his own body and was merely a spectator; a passenger in the car and someone else behind the wheel.

Then he was gone.

Part Three

Cedar

Chapter Twenty-Nine

NOW

I caught a glimpse of myself in the mirror in the lounge above the fireplace and was caught off-guard by the reflection staring back at me. How odd I looked with dreadlocks. So unlike myself. I was half-tempted to cut them off right then and there, but there was a more pressing matter building up inside me.

Looking down at myself I was aghast to see an ill-fitting vest and saggy shorts and quickly went to find something a bit more suitable in my closet.

Riffling through my closet, I decided on a dark blue button-down shirt and a slim-fitting pair of khaki chinos.

These would do nicely.

I grabbed a set of keys from the hook by the door and left.

The air was cooler than I had anticipated, but it didn't matter. There would still be loads of people around tonight. I headed up from the beach and towards town, looking at things with fresh eyes as I walked. The first thing I noticed was the stares I was getting. So different from the looks I was used to. Some with curious eyes, others full of judgement. I didn't care, though. Tonight, I wasn't out to impress. Tonight, I was only after one thing. I knew what my body ached for and I knew exactly where to go to find it.

When I got to MAD bar, the place was moderately crowded but I found a stool by the bar where I sat and ordered a Mai Tai. It didn't take long for the fishes to bite.

Within moments of my drink arriving, someone joined me on my left, lowering himself down on the stool next to me as he checked me out. His gaze lingered on my torso, which filled out the navy shirt more than it normally did, the buttons straining at the seams and hugging the muscles in my arms.

I kept my gaze focused straight ahead at the wall of liquor behind the bar. Sipping my drink nonchalantly as if unaware of his eyes focusing on me.

"*¿Lo que, bebe*?" he asked in an authentic Spanish accent, gesturing to my glass.

I took a moment to respond, enjoying the tension my silence created. He had turned his head to face me now, giving up on playing coy. He leaned against the bar in a seductive post and as I turned my eyes to see him more clearly, I took in his appearance.

"Mai Tai," I responded in my newly gruff voice.

"Oh, you're not Spanish," he said in a tone of apology. I didn't respond. Instead, I allowed myself to drink in the sight of him. How strange a look he was giving me. It was as if his eyes were saying dirty things to me, undressing me almost. Perhaps these were what people called "bedroom eyes."

I didn't think I had ever been regarded in such a way. Like a proper piece of meat. This man didn't care what I did for a living or what my favourite colour was or where I grew up. As I studied his expression. There was only one thing behind his eyes.

Lust.

"My name's Rodriguez," he said to me, offering up his hand.

I didn't respond straight away and I didn't shake what was being presented. Instead I swivelled my chair so that we were face-to-face; profile to profile, and stared him down, a sly smile creeping up on my face. I ran a hand through my long, blond hair and puffed out my chest slightly, giving him a better appreciation of what I had to offer. His eyes followed suit as I hoped they would and before long I found myself standing up, closing in the distance between us until I could smell the scent of his aftershave and feel the heat emanating from his body. He moved back slightly at first, perhaps surprised at my forwardness. I allowed my hand that wasn't clutching my drink to gently graze his arm, just enough so that he felt it.

When his eyes returned to my own, I parted my full lips and ran my tongue across them, moistening them seductively like I had seen done so many times before in the movies.

"You wanna get out of here?" I asked.

But I turned to leave before he could answer, knowing full well that he would follow. As I reached the door, he reached out his strong arm to open it for me in as gentlemanly a way as he could muster.

I smiled to myself as I led the way out of the bar and into the night.

He caught up quickly with me and attempted small talk as I led him towards a part of the beach where I knew we would be alone.

"So, uh, you from around here?"

"Yes," I murmured in response.

"Cool. I, uh, know a place not far from here. Great food. Good music…"

I kept my eyes straight ahead, the destination being the only thing on my mind.

"Or we could go to my place, maybe?" he suggested.

"I've got a better idea…"

He was cute. Very good-looking, actually. Much hotter than any man who would normally give me any attention. My skin tingled all over with anticipation. I enjoyed feeling his eyes on me as we walked, watching my arse that filled out my chinos perfectly, if not making them appear slightly too tight. He wanted me. I knew it. From my peripheral vision, I could see him adjust himself in his jeans as perhaps the thought of what we were about to do danced through his mind.

"Not much of a talker, eh?"

"We're almost there."

We reached the spot I had in mind and I took him by the hand, enjoying the warm sensation of his hand in mine. I led the way down a grassy path, taking care with my footing on the jagged rocks that lined it. With my free hand, I moved branches out of the way from the low-hanging trees that skirted the trail. It was even darker down here now that we were away from any streetlamps and the moon above our heads was our only guide.

"Woah, where we headed?"

I'm sure I could sense a mild tinge of nerves to his voice as he ducked and moved to avoid getting a naked branch square in his eye.

"You sure you know where you're going?"

Definite nerves.

"You're not taking me somewhere so you can kill me, or something, are ya?"

His last sentence stopped me in my tracks. I paused for a minute, his hand still in mine, then turned to face him. "Now why would I do a thing like that?"

His expression, although cast in shadow, darkened and his brow furrowed as he considered the tone of my question. After a second of watching him flounder, I smiled to ease his tension.

He softened immediately and returned my smile, his gaze lingering on my lips. He let go of my hand and cupped my face as he lowered his head to mine for a kiss.

My body felt electric at the sensation of his lips pressed on mine. He was gentle, sensitive, and careful. I let my hands fall limp at my sides and closed my eyes and lost myself in the moment.

The feeling was exquisite. It had been so long since I'd felt longing from a guy. I parted my lips and let my tongue explore his mouth and invited him into mine. He gripped my face gently in his large hands, pulling me closer still until our bodies were pressed up against the other. His erection pressed up against my pelvis. I was growing hard too, lost in the sensation of his tongue licking my own.

It took all the effort I could muster to pull away and turn away from him before he could protest, and continue the last few metres towards the clearing to which we were headed.

"Ah, you tease…" he joked, following closely behind me.

After a few more paces the path opened out into the most beautiful secluded clearing.

"Oh, wow!" he said. "I had no idea this was even here."

It was a small space I had discovered as a child that had remained all but unknown over the years. The gravelly terrain dissipated into a small sandy beach that was sheltered from the low-hanging palm trees and the tall, overgrown grass. The road behind was barely visible and the only light to illuminate the space was the glow from the moon up above, which danced and glittered on the waves in front of us.

"It's gorgeous down here," he said more to me than the surroundings. "How'd you ever find this place?"

But I had had enough of talking. I pulled his face into mine this time, planting my open mouth on his, forcefully yet passionately. He responded by returning my kiss. I explored his muscular arms, running my hands over his broad, rounded shoulders, tracing the bulging lines of his biceps.

He was still hard, as was I; my erection pressed up against my trousers. His hands sunk to my ass, gripping it tightly and squeezing as if testing out the firmness of a melon.

"You've got me fucking horny," he moaned between kisses.

I let my hands explore underneath his shirt and find his abs, brushing over them with my fingertips before gripping onto his waist and drawing him into me even closer.

Then his hands found the dreadlocks and he ran his fingers over them, pulling at my head and forcing my eyes open.

He doesn't want you.

I heard the words come from somewhere in my head. I could feel my expression changing as the truth behind them hit me and the playful lust I was swimming in switched to blind rage.

Stark realisation set in and something deep in my belly snapped. I lashed out, pulling away from his mouth and slapping him across the face as hard as I could, dragging my nails across his cheek until I could feel the hot sensation of blood under my fingers.

"What the fuck!" he shouted as he recoiled from my slap. He grabbed his face as he teetered backward out of shock.

I lashed out again, kneeing him in the groin with all my might. He let out a muffled cry as he fell to the sand, buckled over and curling into a ball.

"You fucking bitch," he groaned through clenched teeth as the feeling no doubt shot up from his crotch to the rest of his body.

Again, I attacked, kicking him in the ribs while he was down.

"You don't want me...Guys never want me. You want Lyric!" I screamed as I kicked him again. "They never want me. They always want *him*!" The tears came now, clouding my vision that had become shrouded in a red mist. "Everyone always wants Lyric. But none of you are good enough for him. *None of you*," I screamed into the night.

I kicked him again and again, before I heard some sort of sickening crack coming from his sides. He was loosening up at my feet, becoming slack beneath my attack, perhaps losing consciousness.

"You're fucking filth. You're scum. You're always attracted to him, but you're never good enough for him."

I sunk to my knees and straddled him, forcing him onto his back by twisting his shoulder away from himself until he was staring up at me through a dazed and pained expression.

"P-please..." he pleaded, spitting out blood and staring up at me.

I reached behind me and grabbed hold of a rock the size of my hand. I raised it above my head.

"Everyone always wants Lyric. Everyone always wants Lyric. When will it be my turn to be noticed? When will boys start to want me? When?"

I brought the rock down on his head, hitting him hard across the cheek. His face whipped to the left as a stream of crimson blood shot from the wound. His head rolled back to neutral, a gaping gash now staring up at me from the impact.

As I held the rock in my hand, there was another shift, as if I could feel myself being pulled away. It was almost magnetic, as if something had gripped me from the shoulders and was yanking me back. I looked down at the blood on my clothes and the rock in my hand and could only watch and observe as the rage melted away into a sort of core-shaking fear like I had never experienced before in my life.

Then I was gone.

Chapter Thirty

Now

"Cedar…" the female detective said as she orchestrated her next approach. "It's nice of you to join us tonight."

The male officer sat back, more taken aback than his partner at having witnessed Lyric's other personality manifest itself before his very eyes. The hairs on the back of his neck were visibly standing on end and he had one hand under the table, presumably close to some panic button in case he felt the need to call for backup.

"You'll have to excuse my colleague," she went on. "He's served on the force with me for over a decade, but when it comes to psychological disturbances, he's as green as they come."

"I wasn't sure he was going to let me through," Cedar whispered, feeling his voice return for the first time in a while. He looked around the room, shaking his head as he realised where he was. "I see our boy Lyric has gotten us into a bit of a pickle…"

"Don't you mean, you *both* have?" she asked, her eyes narrowing.

Cedar's gaze met her own and he assessed her quietly.

"Little old me? Why, whatever do you mean?"

"It seems that whenever you come around, Lyric ends up in trouble."

"Lyric's always been the naughty one…" He studied his hands, turning them over as if seeing them for the first time.

"That's not exactly true, now is it?" The female officer was choosing her words carefully, like talking to a small child so as not to frighten it off. "For instance, the night of the accident…"

Cedar's left eye twitched and he tilted his head as if trying to rid his ear of water.

"I don't want to talk about that…"

"From what we've gathered, there was a bit of an incident that night."

Cedar touched the crown of his head and ran his hands down the length of the blond dreadlocks, taking one in between his fingers and inspecting it with a furrowed brow.

"Do you not remember the man you attacked?"

"Attacked." The word came out of his mouth as though it had a bitter taste.

"Left for dead, actually," the male officer interjected.

"It was lucky for him that there were some passersby who heard all the commotion and came to help," she continued. "They found you, or should I say Lyric, standing over the body of a Rodriguez Sanford, covered in blood and clutching a huge rock. If they hadn't arrived when they did, who knows what you might have done."

"He's alive?"

The female officer made a show of checking her records before answering with a nod. "You put him in a coma for two months."

She must have hoped that her comment would hit him hard, but he just stared at the wall behind them as if in some sort of a trance.

"Cedar, do you know why Lyric got sent away to the Institute in Catalonia?"

"Enlighten me."

"Cedar, your brother was diagnosed with Dissociative Personality Disorder. He displayed multiple personalities. After the incident on the beach, the one you were responsible for, he was deemed too unstable to stand trial and sent to the Institute to undergo intensive psychotherapy. He remained there until, *apparently,* he was released at the age of twenty. If Rodriguez Sanford had died, he might still be there, but the judge was lenient on him, on the proviso that he sought the necessary treatment for his condition."

Both officers studied his expression which remained unchanged; still and unblinking, with only the corner of his lips twitching slightly.

"Apparently, he made such incredible progress during his time there and his condition stabilised in such a manner that his doctors deemed him fit to return to everyday life as long as he continued his therapy sessions and stayed on his meds. But I'd wager that Lyric has stopped taking his meds and that *you,*" she paused, making sure he knew she was referring to Cedar, "have been making more appearances as of late."

"He tries to keep me down. Hidden. But I've always been stronger."

"Cedar...I've got something to tell you and I need to make sure you're listening to me. Are you listening to me?" she asked, waiting for his gaze to make contact with hers before she continued. "You're not *real.*"

Another twitch, this time one that seemed to affect his entire face.

"Did you hear me, Cedar? You're. Not. Real."

His lips were twitching further now, not into a smile, but rather a snarl of sorts.

"You're. Not. Real," she repeated for emphasis, making sure she looked him square in the eye and accentuated each word so he felt the weight behind them.

"Fuck you," he snarled in a tone that was almost otherworldly. His pupils were dilated, making his eyes seem like two vast pools of black.

"You materialised as a way for Lyric to deal with the passing of his brother and family. You died that night in the car along with your mother and father."

"Fuck you. Stop it."

"Lyric was traumatised by the accident; felt responsible for allowing you to drive the car after he had crashed it. He was so deeply hurt by what happened that something inside him snapped. He started speaking like you, acting like you, and even wearing your clothes. It was his brain's way of coping with the guilt and the grief and the loss. But it wasn't something new. It was something he had been dealing with since you both were kids. You know what I'm talking about now?"

He opened his mouth to speak, but then hesitated before finding the words. "He was always a little off..."

"It started with sleepwalking. Waking up in strange places with no memory of how he had gotten there or what he had done. Then as you both grew up he got involved in crimes, drugs...started acting out. There may have even been other personalities, as well, but somehow, he managed to deal with them for a while. They were never really strong enough yet. But after the accident, your accident, the one he felt responsible for, something shifted and he lost control."

Cedar stood to get up, but the male officer was quick and managed to grab hold of his arms. He cuffed Cedar's hands in front of him—for his own protection or Cedar's, he didn't know—and forced him back into his seat.

"*Fuck you, get off me! Get him off me!*" He squirmed and shouted as he was forced back into his chair. But he gave up fighting after a few seconds, knowing it was a losing battle as the male officer dominated him easily in both size and strength.

"But you were strong. You had more power over him. Tell me something, Cedar; why is it you seem to want to see your brother suffer?"

"You don't know what you're talking about."

"Every time you come around you seem to cause trouble for Lyric."

"I love him."

"Do you?"

"Of course, I do. He's my brother. I only want what's best for him."

"Even if that means potentially sending him to prison?"

"Of course not. Why would you say that?"

"Because that's where he's headed, Cedar."

"You're lying."

"Why would you attack Rodriguez Sanford?"

"That filthy thing? He wasn't good enough for my brother. He was scum."

"Not good enough, Cedar?"

"No one is ever good enough for Lyric. No one."

"I think there's more to it than that."

"I'm done talking."

"I think you're jealous."

"That's preposterous."

"Is it? I think you're jealous and that you don't want the best for him at all."

"Shut up."

"You've always been the wallflower, haven't you, Cedar? Always second fiddle to Lyric's charm. His charisma. You never had any of that, did you? And that made you mad. Made you crazy, actually."

"Stop it."

"Always sitting back and watching while Lyric got the guys. While you sat at home, wishing and praying that one day someone would notice you for who you really were and what you had to offer."

Cedar was getting riled up now, and she could tell. His face reddened and he writhed in the chair as if he would implode if he had to sit through any more of this.

"But it never happened, did it, Cedar? Lyric always outshone you in that department. And you died without ever really getting to shine..."

"I hate you. All of you."

"And now this is your way of getting back at him. Now that you've got power over him you can have your moment. You can finally see what it's like to *be* your brother. Have his looks, his charisma. But it didn't really work for you, did it? You may have thought it was what you wanted, but it started working against you when you realised they didn't want *you*. They wanted Lyric. They always have."

"Stop it. Please." He raised his cuffed hands as close to his ears as he could in an attempt to block out her words. "I can't listen to this anymore. Please."

"So you'd get angry with them. Just like you got angry with Rodriguez Sanford."

His shoulders were heaving with silent tears as he dropped his head and looked down at his feet.

"But not every guy was as lucky as Sanford, were they? There were times when you weren't interrupted like you were with him on the beach. Three other times, in fact."

"Please stop..." he murmured.

"Tell us about Lenox, Cedar."

There, she'd said it. Her ace in the hole. The name she must have been withholding for precisely the right minute, knowing the effect it would have on him.

And sure enough, it did. He stopped squirming and looked her dead in the eye for the first time in minutes, his face red and blotchy and his eyes glazed.

"Lenox..." he repeated back to her, the name rolling off his tongue and lingering in the air between them.

Chapter Thirty-One

THEN

As the iPhone screen unlocked itself with a swipe of Lenox's finger, he instantly regretted it. He always hated it when his ex used to creep in his phone, checking his pictures and texts. It screamed distrust and Lenox had always promised himself he would never betray someone else's privacy like that.

But sitting there in Lyric's bed, with his phone unattended, he began to realise that perhaps he had some trust issues after all. He listened for Lyric in the toilet to gauge how much time he had to snoop, and before he knew it he had clicked on the pictures icon. An album list displayed itself for his choosing.

Scrolling through, he saw one dated a couple of days ago. When he opened the album, hundreds of miniature thumbnails came up on the screen; a load of crowd shots from the beach or somewhere sunny, the blue skies unmistakable even from the tiny squared images. He enlarged one and studied it intently, his mind working to make sense of what his eyes were telling him.

It was a group shot of Lenox and his friends on the beach.

Odd. I don't remember that being taken.

A swipe to the right revealed a second snap from another angle, just far away enough for the photographer to be inconspicuously out of eyeshot. Another swipe revealed a picture with a different date; with only Lenox and Bambi in the shot. Again, the picture seemed to be taken from a slight distance down the beach, so far away he had to pinch the picture to zoom in and make out their figures. But it was them. Sure as anything.

Another swipe revealed a group of people in a dimly lit room, dining from what he could make out.

It was that night at Las Dos Lunas.

Lyric was there?

The next one was another group shot of all of them that night on the beach. Just before they spotted Lyric in the water.

Lenox's heart was in his throat, beating like a snare drum in his ears. The blood circulating through his body throbbed a similar rhythmic drumming in his temples as he continued flicking through the pictures.

Each and every one was of him or one of his friends. Hundreds of them. All taken without Lenox or any of the others being aware.

Lyric's been following me. But why?

He turned his attention back to the toilet and he could hear the tap running now, but it didn't stop him. He was like a thing possessed.

The beach. Dinners they'd had. Their villa. Close-up pictures of the front of their apartment. Them arriving from the airport.

How the fuck?

His mind was reeling as he exited the photos and clicked on the green messages icon. He recognised his own number at the top of the first message. As soon as he clicked on it, he wished he hadn't.

Stay away from him.

The words were plastered across the screen in the blue message box.

Jesus Christ. It was the text he had gotten on the beach that first night with Lyric.

It was sent *from* Lyric.

Stay away from him.

Why would Lyric send that to him? And how? It didn't make any sense. How would he have even had his number that first night? They had only just met...

But then realisation dawned on him as the chips slowly began to fall into place before his wide-open eyes.

He had lost his phone. On the beach. Lyric had found it. He must have gotten his number that way.

But why would Lyric send Lenox a text warning Lenox to stay away from him?

Seconds passed as the wheels in his head turned so loudly he could almost hear the sound of them working. He racked his brain trying to make sense of what he had just seen.

Then he smelled the vanilla.

Sweet and yet so pungent. The same scent he had smelled the first night he and Lyric had sex. It was so strong it forced his gaze up from the phone.

The sight of Lyric's broad frame standing motionless in the doorframe made him jump.

"Jesus," he cried out in surprise.

But Lyric didn't move. He just stood there, still, his face shrouded in shadows, his hands hanging limply at his sides.

"Lyric…" he began, not knowing where he was prepared to take the conversation.

Lyric took a step out of the shadows, revealing his face. It was twisted into a scowl of some sort, as if he had just smelled something horrible and was investigating the source.

"Your phone…" Lenox's gaze dropped to the iPhone in his hand as though he was unsure how it had gotten there.

"Are you looking through *his* phone?" Lyric asked, his voice more mocking in tone than upset.

Lenox was surprised to hear that voice coming from Lyric. It sounded different. Deeper. Grittier somehow.

"I'm sorry. I…" He couldn't disguise his confusion. "Your phone was beeping. And then…"

"I had a bad feeling about you right from the beginning."

Lyric's words seemed to tumble quietly from his open mouth, as if he had said them all before.

"What did you just say?"

"I tried to tell him, but as always…" He took another step closer.

There was something off-putting about his stance. He reminded Lenox of a predator preparing to battle a foe for food. His body had taken on a different shape, bent over slightly and almost menacing in stature.

Lenox slowly pulled himself out of bed, still clutching the phone in his hand.

"Lyric, why…?"

"Stop calling me that," he interrupted, his jaw clenched and his hands balling into fists at his side.

"Calling you what?"

"Lyric." The word was spat out as if he couldn't handle the taste of it on his lips.

Lenox furrowed his brow in confusion, looking once again at the phone in his hand as if it held the answers to all his questions. "Have you been following me?"

"I told him you were just like all the others. I always tell him. Always have."

"You've been following me," he repeated. This time the words came out as a statement rather than a question. "You've been following all of us. Since we got here...But, why?"

"I always try and warn him about you all. I don't know why he won't see...One day, he'll learn his lesson."

Lyric was staring at the wall behind him, his eyes wide and manic. It was as if he was having a conversation with someone else who wasn't in the room. Lenox regarded him cautiously, like a mouse would eye up a cat coming face-to-face. As Lyric took a step forward, Lenox took one back, retreating to the far wall inch by inch, his body quivering as his instinct for self-preservation kicked in.

"Lyric, you're scaring me. And that text, telling me to stay away." He swallowed hard. "It came from you?"

He wrapped his arms around himself for protection.

"You needed to be told. I needed to put you in your place. Quickly. But you didn't listen, did you?"

"What do you mean, put me in my place? What is this all about?"

"Why is it never *me* that anybody wants?"

"What are you talking about?"

"It's always been Lyric. He always gets all the attention."

"I don't...I don't understand." His back was pressed up against the wall now. The brick was cold on his naked back and it didn't help the shivers that were snaking through him.

"And they're never good enough for him. They're always trash. All of them. Sluts. Just like you."

"Excuse me?"

"Just once, I wish it could be me they want. Notice me. Not him. What about me? When's it going to be my turn to be happy?"

Lenox stared at him for a moment, dumbfounded. Something was off. Very off.

This wasn't the man he was just lying in bed next to. *Whoever* this was, was someone else.

"Lyric...I think maybe we should talk. Sit down. Maybe I could–maybe I could call someone for you..." Lenox began, the reality and potential seriousness of the situation coming to light in his eyes.

"There's no one to call," he answered flatly, closing the distance between them even further until they were only metres apart.

"This isn't you. What's wrong? You're scaring me."

"You should be scared."

A moment passed between them, their eyes locked on one another like deer caught in the headlights of an oncoming car, then Lyric shot out his hands and gripped around Lenox's neck.

And squeezed.

Lenox didn't have time to react. He reached his hands up to try to peel Lyric's off him, but Lyric's grip was like a vice around his neck. He instantly lost his breath as Lyric choked him, squeezing tighter and tighter.

His eyes were forced open, wide as saucers and filled with terror, and locked on Lyric. Petrified confusion gripped him as Lyric, or whoever this was, stared back at him with a crazed and maniacal look that was at once fury and disgust personified. His teeth were gritted and every muscle in his body seemed tensed and focused on crushing Lenox's neck.

He fought back uselessly, clawing and scratching at Lyric's hands, reaching around to try to push his face away, find his eyes and put pressure on his sockets. But everything seemed useless as he fought for his life. The room went silent, all except for the strangled cries escaping from Lenox's lips. He spat and dribbled as the life was squeezed out of him. His eyelids drooped and his body softened as he began to lose hope and, silently, give up.

For a moment, it seemed that Lyric's grip was growing tired. It loosened for a split-second, which was just long enough for Lenox to come back to life and wriggle free. He reached his arm around with all his might and dug his thumb into Lyric's eye, driving it as far into the socket as he could, forcing Lyric to recoil backwards, a growl emanating from his twisted mouth.

Lenox was free.

He sprang into action, despite being deprived of oxygen, and flew around the bed for the door to the room. But Lyric was quick and was on him before he could reach the door. He grabbed him and shoved him onto the bed. Lenox hit his skull hard on the wooden bed frame with a sickening thwack. For a second, he was dazed and could only lie there, arms splayed out at his sides as he watched Lyric climb on top of him, straddling his waist and raising something metallic in the air above him. As Lyric paused for a second, Lenox's eyes refocused enough to recognise the object as a huge kitchen knife, the thick blade gleaming in the light from the moon outside.

"I warned you to stay away," he muttered in a voice so quiet it could almost be misinterpreted as soothing, before bringing the blade down in one strong swipe, over his head and straight into Lenox's heart.

Lenox wasn't sure if he cried out or not. There was nothing in his ears but white silence and nothing in his body but a sudden, incredible wet warmth as his life trickled away.

An emotionless second passed. Then time seemed to stand still as all thoughts but one drained from his mind.

I'm dying.

Lenox's limbs felt non-existent and he could do nothing more than look up and glimpse his attacker, standing above him; his once beautiful features now twisted into an evil grimace, and dreadlocks streaked, splattered, and stained with crimson blood.

He watched as Lyric's once brilliant blue eyes grew darker and clouded over. And as the heavy scent of vanilla began to fade and dissipate, he gave in and let his eyes blur and close.

Chapter Thirty-Two

NOW

The room grew oddly quiet for the first time in hours. Even the hum of the air conditioning seemed to still out of respect. Lyric's head drooped once again as he seemingly came back into the room, his body language betraying his silence as if he took responsibility for the truth that had finally been told.

Cedar was gone, but the reverberations of his words could still be felt by all those in the room. Lyric shuddered and cradled his restrained hands to his chest, shielding his heart like a child for protection from the horrible monsters who lived under his bed. As he returned, the cloud that hung over his mind burned away and he took heed of his whereabouts once more.

After a moment of silence, where he allowed his breath to return to normal, he finally had the courage to raise his head and peer out at the officers from under his long lashes.

Both were staring at him intently, their expressions stern but tinged with something that he couldn't quite make out.

Was it concern? But why would officers of the law show any sort of concern for a convicted criminal?

His gaze drifted from the man to the woman, lingering for a moment on each, studying their expressions and trying to gauge something from them.

The woman was the first to move, shuffling papers together and replacing photographs into their pristine manila envelopes that had been placed to one side. When she had meticulously tidied her area, she exchanged glances with the man to her side, their eyes speaking a silent language. He responded with a slight nod of his head.

Lyric's gaze continued to dart from one to the other, waiting for one of them to act. There was something strange about the way they were regarding him, as if there had been a shift in the room that he hadn't noticed and the dynamic had changed. The more he stared at them the more nervous he got. He studied their faces. Stern and yet emotionless as if they were trying their best to remain neutral and unfazed in his presence. But there was something more. Something he couldn't quite place.

Something almost...clinical, about them and the way in which they now sat.

The rhythmic beating of his heart that had just returned to normal began to spike as if it had realised something that had eluded him until now. From nowhere, a question appeared in his mind, like a light bulb switching on in a dimly lit room, illuminating a sudden doubt that he hadn't considered before.

It took him a moment to formulate the question in his head before his lips could figure out how to ask it.

"I never did ask to see your badges..." he murmured, his voice hesitant and unsure.

The man and woman shifted slightly in their seats, a movement so subtle it would have been unmistakable to the untrained eye. But Lyric had become quite masterful at reading people's body language, and theirs spoke volumes of awkwardness and discomfort.

There was another brief, silent exchange between the two before they returned their eyes to Lyric, brows slightly furrowed. It was the man who spoke first this time.

"Badges?" he asked. The word lingered in the air around Lyric like a fly he couldn't quite swat. "What sort of badges should we have, Lyric?"

The question carried more weight than it should have and it forced Lyric to sit up straighter than before. He laughed to himself at the ridiculousness of the question, for the answer seemed like it should be fairly obvious to them all.

He opened his mouth to speak but stopped himself when he realised that the man and woman didn't share the humour he detected behind the question. The man looked once again to the woman, who had now sat back in her chair and crossed her legs almost too casually, as if her work here was done.

"Lyric," he began, choosing his words with obvious care, like one would if trying to explain something fairly complicated to a child, "do you know where you are?"

Again, it was Lyric's turn to guffaw at the ludicrousness of the question.

Of course, he knew where he was. He smiled but couldn't quite find the words to answer. Then he looked around the room, as if seeing it for the first time.

Somehow things looked different than he had previously thought. There was no two-way mirror as he had sworn there had been upon entering, or table with a coffee maker and mugs. The room was simple. Stark. White. Brighter than he remembered, with only a lone camera mounted on the wall pointing directly at him, a tiny red light illuminated on its side.

He returned his gaze to the man and woman before him.

"Of course, I do. I'm at the police station..." But as the words left his lips, he wasn't so sure anymore.

The man offered a tight-lipped smile at him, not one of amusement but more of pity or concern. The woman remained unfazed by Lyric's admission, and continued to stare blank-faced at him.

"Lyric, you know you're not at the police station," the man said, enunciating each word with much more careful consideration than he had before.

"What do you mean? Of course, I am. You called me in..." Once more, his sentence was drenched with uncertainty. He laughed to himself as he looked them both in the eye.

But after a moment, he noticed something he hadn't registered before. He glanced down to the officer's clothing and his mouth opened into a silent "o" shape as his pulse began to thump away inside his head, beating his temples as panic began to rise inside his throat.

The officers weren't wearing police uniforms. They were wearing white coats.

Doctor's coats.

Crisp. White. Clinical doctor's coats. Clipped to the breast pockets of each were identity badges displaying a photo as well as a name and title. Lyric's gaze lingered over each in turn, trying to make sense of why officers of the law would be dressed in doctor's coats, like they worked in some sort of...

Hospital.

The panic was getting stronger now, gripping his throat like a noose and sucking all the moisture out of his mouth to leave behind a sandy-like grit on his tongue.

"Lyric, my name is Doctor Powell," the man said, "and this is Doctor Sanchez." He pointed to the woman at his side. "I am the Superintendent here and Doctor Sanchez is the lead psychotherapist of the long-term care ward of L'Institut Pere Mata."

He paused then, letting his words hit Lyric like pellets from a BB gun; sharp and stinging, leaving his skin hot and itchy like he was on fire.

"Does that help you remember?"

The woman, Doctor Sanchez, sat forward and put her hand gently on Doctor Powell's arm as a way of shifting the power of the dialogue back to her. When she spoke again, her voice was softer, gentler, the way a mother would speak to her newborn child.

"Lyric, I don't want you to start to worry. First off, let me begin by reassuring you that you're safe. You're here, with us, and this is a safe place."

Lyric's eyes were blurring as the familiar prickle of tears began. His mouth was ajar and a thousand thoughts were trickling through his head like drips from a leaky faucet.

"I...I don't understand. I thought..."

"We don't expect you to understand, Lyric. I'm so sorry we had to put you through all of this. But I'm afraid Doctor Powell needed to see for himself to judge the progress you've been making."

"Progress?" he asked, his voice small and insignificant.

"Yes, Lyric. Progress," she repeated. "Lyric, this may come as a shock to you, but I'm afraid you need to keep hearing the truth."

Her voice softened even further as if she didn't wish to frighten him with what she was about to say next.

"Lyric, you remember coming to stay at the Institute after your parents' death, don't you?"

He nodded slightly, sucking back tears and wiping at his sore, burning eyes.

"After your parents and brother died in the accident you were picked up on the beach not far from your family home. The reason you don't recall any specific details about what occurred with Rodriguez Sanford was because I believe you had an episode after the accident which is when your Dissociative Identity Disorder, or multiple personalities if you will, officially began to manifest itself."

Lyric squirmed in his seat, his skin crawling as if he had been dipped in a tank full of insects and they were slowly worming their way around his body.

"In the recollection of events you just gave to us, you were released from the hospital two years after first being sentenced, thanks to the progress you'd made and your good behaviour. Do you remember that?"

Both doctors exchanged another telling look.

"Yes...Of course, I do. I was twenty when I got out."

"Lyric, do you know how old you are now?"

Lyric was getting angry at having to answer all these stupid questions.

"Why are you asking me all this? What does my age have to do with anything?"

"Lyric, if you wouldn't mind just answering the question," Doctor Sanchez implored gently.

He let out a grunt of disapproval, his gaze shifting from one doctor to the other, the feeling of unease becoming stronger with each passing second.

"I'm twenty-eight, of course."

The puzzled look the doctors returned to him made his hands tremble.

"Lyric, I'm afraid I've got something to tell you, and it is going to come as a bit of a shock."

"What? What is it?"

"Lyric...You're not twenty-eight years old."

"What? What do you mean? Of course, I am...I think I know how old I am, for Chrissake. What are you talking about?"

"No. Lyric, you're not. I'm afraid you're almost forty."

"What? Don't be ridiculous. What are you talking about?"

"You've been in the hospital for nearly twelve years now."

"No. Come on, that's crazy." His gaze darted around the room as he considered what she had just said. "Come on. That's ridiculous. Forty? That's insane. I'm not forty. I'm twenty-eight. My birthday was like, six months ago. Why would you think..."

Doctor Sanchez was silent for a moment.

"I'm afraid not, Lyric. You've been a patient here in the long-term care ward for almost twelve years."

"That's impossible. That's impossible. Why would you say that? Why are you lying to me? How could I be...No, that's insane. What is this all about?"

"I wish I were lying, Lyric. You tell me this exact story you've just recounted to us every week when we meet for your sessions. We've been meeting, you and I, every week since you were first admitted. And every week we go through this same discussion. I've been trying to get through to you for almost twelve years now."

Lyric could only stare now, his gaze flicking frantically around the room like an insect.

"What are you saying? That I've been in a hospital for...No. I can't listen to this...When do you think I got here, then?" His voice strained to sound sarcastic as if he were entertaining what they were telling him.

"Lyric, you were picked up...By the police. It was late June in 2016. Do you remember what happened that year?"

"Of course, I remember, because it just fucking happened! It is June 2016! What's wrong with you both?"

The panic in his voice showed itself as the threads in his mind unravelled.

The doctors shared another all-knowing glance and Doctor Powell gave another very thin-lipped smile, casting his eyes down to the papers on the table.

"Lyric, the year is 2028. I know you don't understand what's happening, and I'm so sorry to have to tell you this. But you need to start listening. You've been in this hospital for twelve years. Ever since the police found you near one of your parents' apartments, in the early morning hours of Friday, June 28th, 2016."

"That was only fucking yesterday. Why are you saying these things?"

Doctor Sanchez drew in a deep breath through clenched teeth, clearly determined to plough on.

"You were found roaming the streets, as if in a daze." She paused, choosing her words carefully. "Covered in blood."

Now, his eyes focused on hers.

"Blood?" he repeated back to her.

"You were picked up quickly and brought in for questioning. They couldn't get anything out of you. You were unresponsive, completely blank behind the eyes as if in a trance. The officers who picked you up couldn't get any answers. When they checked your record, they came across the hospital files of your time at the Institut Pere Mata, and a specialist was called in. It wasn't long before they checked the address we had on file for you. And that's when they found..." Her voice cracked, as if it hurt her to speak the next words that came out of her mouth. "That's when they found the body of Lenox Winter."

"Lenox..."

"He had been stabbed multiple times in the chest and was pronounced dead at the scene."

"Lenox is..."

"Your fingerprints were all over the body and the blood on yourself was a match to the DNA of the victim."

"Lenox is dead...Fuck...Oh, Jesus..."

"It's okay, Lyric. It's okay."

"What the fuck do you mean it's okay? Of course, it's not okay. What are you saying to me...?"

His whole frame vibrated with fury and his eyes went wide, like those of an animal snared in a trap.

"I was the doctor that was called down to the island to complete a full psychological evaluation upon your arrest. You were unfit to stand trial and were sent here. To the Institut Pere Mata, where you have been a patient ever since."

She sat back after finishing, braced, as if she understood the effect her words were going to have on him and she could watch their impact play out on his features. His lips moved as if he was speaking but without any words they could detect.

A single tear fell from his eye as the weight of the revelations he had just suffered began to take its effect.

"I'm so sorry, Lyric..."

But her apology carried only minimal sincerity.

"Doctor Powell is here to revisit your case and judge the effectiveness of your current dosage of chlorpromazine. I've been hoping we might be able to lower it this trimester, but I'm fairly certain this will be refuted. Your delusions are as strong today as they were when you joined us."

Her words were like liquid lava, pouring over him and searing his skin. He put his head in his hands and gently pounded at his temples in frustration as the truth of what she was telling him began to sink in.

He grabbed hold of his hair, expecting to entangle his hands in his long dreadlocks.

Only they weren't there.

"What the fuck?" he shouted as he patted his head in search of his long hair, but was only greeted with a tightly shorn buzz cut. He kneaded his skull and plucked at the short hairs with his fingers, desperately searching for something that wasn't there.

"My dreads?" he called out, his voice seized with panic.

"Lyric, you had those cut off when you first arrived at the Institute. They were a safety risk to you. We were afraid you might use their length to harm yourself in some way."

"This isn't happening. This can't be happening. I'm only here being questioned. I...I need to go home. Right now. *Now*!" he shouted, panic-stricken and unable to fathom what was happening. His skin crawled and his heart pounded in his chest as his vision blurred and hearing softened, all sounds being dulled to a white noise.

"Lyric...You are home."

But as he was refuting their apparent lies, his whole body gripped with fear and hysteria, desperate to flee the situation and get as far away from there as he could, something gave way in his mind. A small part of him started to lend itself to the idea that perhaps they might be telling the truth.

Doctor Sanchez reached down into a bag at her side that Lyric hadn't noticed before and pulled out what appeared to be a small, round hand mirror. She carefully opened it and turned the reflective side so that he could peer into the looking glass.

It took him a moment for his eyes to refocus, but as he wiped at the tears that clouded his vision, someone stared back at him in the mirror that he almost didn't recognise. He opened his mouth to speak, but there were no words to explain the emotions he was feeling. All he could do was stare in despair at what he saw in the mirror.

He looked so different. So much older. His long, blond hair was gone; shaved into a closely cropped style that was like a shadow circling his round skull. His eyes seemed sunken and his face withdrawn. Even his skin looked different. Older. There were tiny lines around his eyes that he hadn't had before and the short hair at his temples had started to grey. He angled his face differently as if he was testing the reality of what he was seeing, wondering if the reflection would mirror his movements. As he tilted his head this way and that, so did the stranger who stared back at him. After a moment of silence, he closed his eyes and tore himself away from the mirror, collapsing into his hands and beginning to sob.

"Lyric, we have this conversation almost every week. And every time we reach the end, I have to reveal the truth to you again and again. Lenox, and his murder, and your time here. From what I've gathered, your subconscious built up a wall around itself after Lenox's death, perhaps as a way of protecting itself, or as a way of grieving over what you did. Your mind seems to be on some sort of a loop, living in a constant cycle of denial. It's as if you aren't able to process any new memories. There are many documented cases of such an amnesic state occurring to patients after suffering a traumatic loss of some kind. But I must admit, the fact that your subconscious seems to be stuck somehow, repeating the same scenario over and over again, as if in some cyclical state of regression, is disconcerting, even considering your previous diagnosis. Just when I think we're getting close to a breakthrough, either with your medicines or through our sessions, your brain seems to reset itself again and we're back to square one. Suddenly, in your mind it's twelve years ago. As if no time has passed…"

A moment went by and the white noise softened as Lyric calmed down once again, the panic fleeting and his senses returning to normal. He drew in a deep breath and began his counting down from ten, as he had been taught all those years ago. Another deep breath relaxed him further until his hands stopped shaking and his heartbeat slowed. He glanced up at the two doctors before him.

"But it feels like only yesterday…"

It was the first sign of any sort of acceptance on his part. His words came out pained and full of strain.

Doctor Sanchez paused for a moment, reaching across the table and taking his restrained hands in her own. The touch of her skin was warm on his cold, numb hands, and he appreciated the change in temperature.

"I know it does, Lyric…" After a moment, her hands loosened on his as the truth began to settle around him. He closed his eyes for a moment and tried to centre himself in the room, letting the truth cascade over him like the waves in the sea.

His settled mind, as much as he fought it, at last considered things from their perspective.

"I…I don't remember…"

"I know you don't, Lyric. I'm so, so sorry for all of this. It comes as such a shock to you every time. But that is the case with Dissociative Identity Disorder. After your parents died and the attack on Rodriguez Sanford when you were eighteen, you were in a catatonic state. Completely unresponsive to any sort of treatment or stimulus. And you remained in this state for two weeks."

"Two weeks?"

"I'm afraid so. When you awoke, you were convinced you were Cedar."

"Cedar..."

"It seemed that you had adopted his personality after the accident, presumably as the brain's way of coping with the trauma of losing your family. It wasn't until about a month after you awoke from catatonia that we saw your true self begin to take control again. Whenever Cedar is allowed to take over, he seems to want to punish you somehow. He has been creating elaborate stories about you for years, trying to get you into trouble and make you pay for the way you treated him. He still thinks he's alive and a completely separate entity to you. You've told me before that you and Cedar weren't like normal twins; sometimes inseparable, at other times vying for attention and acting in a confrontational manner towards each other. When you adopted his personality after his death it was as if your subconscious wanted you to suffer, as if you felt you deserved the pain somehow, and it used Cedar to deliver it. The truth is, Lyric, you've never forgiven yourself for the deaths of your parents and Cedar, and these personalities are your brain's way of coping with grief."

"How is it that I keep forgetting?"

"Unfortunately, that's something we have yet to figure out or properly treat. When you were released from the hospital the first time, you were doing so well. Your meds were working and you showed promise of being able to lead a fairly normal life. You were checking into your appointments, and had taken over the running of your parents' café. Things seemed good. And then, eight years later, around the time you would have first met Lenox Winter, things seemed to get worse again. You went off the radar for a while, not showing up for your appointments as often, not renewing your prescriptions..."

She wrung her hands for a moment and Lyric could detect a slight pain in her mannerisms.

"I blame myself for not seeing the signs sooner. For not detecting that your condition was worsening again. Perhaps if I had, then Lenox..."

But there was no use in finishing her sentence.

"After the death of Lenox Winter, when you were picked up by police, you slipped into this amnesiac state, perhaps due to the psychological trauma you experienced, and despite our efforts to pull you out, your brain seems to revert back each time, resetting itself somehow as a way of protecting the psyche from the truth of what has happened to you. And the truth behind what you've done."

"I wish this wasn't happening..."

"I know you do, Lyric. Again, I wish things were different for you."

"Why did you do this today? Why did you let me believe...?"

"I'm afraid this is how most of our sessions begin. Your brain somehow convinces yourself that you've been called in for questioning and our therapy sessions continue from there. I'm sorry we had to play along today, but it was the only way for Doctor Powell to experience first-hand the state in which you remain."

"We believe that it was Cedar's personality that was present and responsible for the death of Lenox Winter, as well as the disappearance and possible death of another three individuals on the island, whose cases remain open to this day," Doctor Powell added. "The particulars of all four cases share some obvious similarities; all males under the age of thirty, all disappearing within a three-mile radius of one another and all frequenting the same bar where *you* had been reported on numerous occasions, as well as where you—or *Cedar*, I should say—allegedly picked up Rodriguez Sanford. Unfortunately, no bodies were ever recovered from the three previous cases, and due to your apparent amnesiac state, I'm not sure we'll ever be able to uncover the truth behind their whereabouts. I fear that if things had gone differently, then the body of Lenox Winter would also have gone undiscovered and his case unsolved."

Doctor Powell sighed deeply, his mouth hardening again into that familiar tight-lipped expression. "I'm afraid at this time we may have to think about exploring a different course of treatment," he continued, his gaze turning towards Doctor Sanchez.

The doctors both stopped for a moment and exchanged yet another expression between themselves before Doctor Powell pushed his chair back. He looked to the camera on the wall, nodded his head in its direction, and stood up.

"I think that's enough for today."

And with that he nodded towards Doctor Sanchez.

Lyric looked up at the same time as he stood, unsure as to what was happening. Doctor Powell passed Doctor Sanchez a piece of paper, which Lyric assumed had his diagnosis scrolled across. She took it, scanned it quickly, and nodded, not once making eye contact.

"Thank you, Doctor Sanchez. Lyric..." Doctor Powell nodded in his general direction, although he avoided Lyric's stare.

After a moment, the door was unlocked from the outside and an official-looking man in uniform escorted Doctor Powell out of the room, leaving Lyric and the head psychotherapist alone for a moment.

She stared him straight in the eye, her arms folded neatly on the table in front of her. She let another moment pass in silence before she attempted conversation again.

"Lyric. Do you need more time?"

He almost laughed out loud at the question.

"More time. More time for what?"

"To process. To think. To remember..."

"I'm not sure I want to remember anything more."

"I understand."

It was her turn to clear her throat and signal to the camera on the wall that she was through. She stood abruptly, gathered the envelopes from the table, and moved towards the doorway before turning back once more to face Lyric who remained seated, small and insignificant at the table.

"Lyric, I'm going to process Doctor Powell's diagnosis and we will commence a new course of treatment tomorrow morning. I will have Dickens escort you back to your room, and I will see you for our next session next week. Do you understand?"

Her voice had changed once again, from soft and kind to formal and sterile. The door opened with a jarring sound and with a final nod to Lyric, she disappeared down the hall.

Lyric was alone now, with nothing but his disturbing thoughts to comfort him.

His eyes remained fixed on a spot on the table until the aforementioned orderly made his way into the room and put a heavy, strong hand on his shoulder.

"It's time," was all he needed to say to let Lyric know he was able to return to his cell, or room, as they called it.

He stood and followed the orderly out of the room.

The hallway was white, with blindingly bright fluorescent bulbs lining the way. A sterile smell of bleach infiltrated his nostrils as he shuffled slowly along the cold, white-tiled floor. As he walked, he noticed the soft slippers that adorned his feet and the grey sweatpants and sweater he wore on top. He let his hands find his head once more, running them softly over his shaved head and silently missing the comfort that his long dreadlocks used to provide.

Things in his mind were becoming clearer now as the details of his life returned to his consciousness. He wasn't sure how long he'd be able to hold on to them this time, but for the time being he let them all wash over him.

After a few minutes of walking along winding hallways and passing nurses and doctors, each nodding hello in Lyric's direction, they reached a large grey door with a small gilded window and large slot in the centre.

The orderly took out a hefty keyring that was attached to his belt and found the appropriate key with which to unlock the heavy padlocked door. The deadbolt slid back and the door creaked open. He motioned for Lyric to lift his wrists. Once he had, the orderly unlocked his restraints and stepped back for Lyric to go inside.

Epilogue

LYRIC STUDIED THE room around him. Sitting on the small, single bed he listened carefully for any noises, but was greeted with a surprisingly comforting silence. The four white walls were slightly padded and the only furniture was the bed and a simple desk and chair. Red, dying tulips sat in a plastic vase filled with dirty water in the centre of the desk, alongside a small black notepad and pen.

A small south-facing window with iron bars across it was the focus of the far wall, and it let in the bright afternoon sunshine. He closed his eyes for a moment and felt the warm rays on his skin.

When he opened his eyes, they drifted to the half dozen or so pictures that were taped to the padded wall above the desk. Standing, he went to investigate.

Each photograph was a picture of his family. His parents. One of Cedar on his own when he was younger. Another of him and his brother down on the beach, arms around each other and enormous grins plastered across their faces. Then a couple of the whole family.

Together. Alive. Content. Safe.

Happy moments captured in time. As he gazed over each, taking in the details of the pictures and feeling the emotions that rose as the memories surfaced, he was filled with an odd sense of ease. If he closed his eyes now, he could still hear his brother calling his name like that day on the beach. He could still feel the soft embrace of his mother when he was sad and needed comforting, and he could still hear the strong, hearty sound of his father laughing as he enjoyed the sight of his boys playing nicely together. He ran his fingers over the photographs, and stayed there in their memory for as long as he could bear until the tears blurred his vision and he started to sob.

About the Author

Joey Jameson lives in Brighton, UK; a world of decadence, glamour, and intrigue. He believes life is better when drizzled with naughtiness and drenched in layer upon layer of sparkling glitter. His work is best appreciated with a hard drink and the lights down low and will leave you wondering just what goes on in that twisted little mind of his.

He is the author of *Candy from Strangers, Blackout, Twisted, Interview with the Porn Star* and *Dirty Talk*.

Stay tuned for more scintillating work to come your way soon...

Email: misterjoeyjameson@gmail.com

Website: www.joeyjameson.com

Twitter: @joeyjameson

Facebook: www.facebook.com/joeyjamesonauthor

Instagram: @joeyjameson

Other books by this author

Dirty Talk

Luca DiIorio begins his freshman year at Cornell, while his boyfriend, Chyna Davidson, embarks on a modeling career based out of Manhattan, New York. Although Luca is only a five-hour drive away, he may as well be on another planet. Having watched Chyna's back for years, Luca struggles with the separation. His new roommate, Zeb Araneda, lends an ear, and a solid friendship is born, but it doesn't keep Luca from worrying.

Chyna learns to navigate the ups and downs of the modeling industry on his own. However, this proves difficult with Luca micromanaging everything, from Chyna's diet to his choice in a roommate. After rejecting several candidates, Chyna and Luca decide on fellow model, Alex Boulet, who turns out to be perfect in more ways than one.

An unexpected appearance raises a multitude of concerns, and the entire family—Lil, Grier, Clark, Jody, and Chip—descend upon the young couple to offer their help. Will Luca and Chyna weather the storm or succumb to pressure from multiple fronts?

A NineStar Press Publication

Published by NineStar Press
P.O. Box 91792,
Albuquerque, New Mexico, 87199 USA.
www.ninestarpress.com

Through My Own Lens

ISBN: 978-1-947904-19-4

Printed in the USA
First Edition
November, 2017

Also available in eBook

ISBN: 978-1-947904-18-7

Warning: This book contains sexually explicit content, which may only be suitable for mature readers.